GW00544235

CAUT

*Reading this book causes
extreme stimulation, lust
and exquisite languor.*

Brought to you by

Indigo After Dark

an Imprint of

Genesis Press, Inc.

Indigo After Dark

is published by

Genesis Press, Inc.
315 Third Avenue North
Columbus, MS 39701

Indigo After Dark, Vol. V
Ebony Butterfly

First Edition

Indigo After Dark, Vol. V
Ebony Butterfly

by
Delilah Dawson

Genesis Press, Inc.

To my husband, Endless thanks for all
the love and support.
To Judy A., crit partner extraordinaire.
Thanks!

Chapter 1

Sharonda Williams frowned as she leaned against the living room wall of her new San Diego apartment. The room was currently a mess, but worth every dime. It was a shame that in the two weeks since she'd moved into the small complex, she was still pretty much living out of the boxes she'd painstakingly lugged up the two stories.

But today she was tired for another reason altogether. She'd searched everywhere but still couldn't find her precious diary, and that was really beginning to worry her. The nightly ritual of writing down her thoughts had become an outlet for her frustrations, personal confessions and intimate fantasies.

As the days went by and the diary remained missing, it felt as if the words were backing up in her head, waiting for the moment when she would open to a blank page and allow the thin, midnight blue pen to bleed her thoughts into ink-scratched sentences.

Sharonda sighed, leaning against the wall and looking out where the balcony curtain was parted to where the moon hung with the flourish of a New Orleans street light. Below, the soft glow clearly revealed the shiny surface of the swimming pool shared by the complex. The shrubs surrounding it offered minimal privacy. Across the way were two apartments. The oddly angled brick building provided her a view into them.

With mild curiosity, she watched as the sliding glass door moved on the downstairs apartment and the elderly Mrs. Benson let her orange cat out for the night. Just as she closed the sliding door and extinguished her light, lights in the upstairs apartment came on.

Immediately Sharonda dimmed hers, then walked to the side table drawer next to the living room couch and retrieved a pair of binoculars. Hurrying back to her previous position, she raised them to her eyes and began to spy into the lit apartment beyond, grateful that the man rarely closed his curtains.

"Oh, yeah," she murmured. The tall black man was usually dressed in a neat executive suit and was always meticulously clean. As he closed the door, she focused close enough to see the gleam of his cleanshaved head. When he placed the briefcase, as usual, on the side table, she took a quick assessment of him, letting the binoculars travel downwards. Goodness, but he had a professional appeal that was downright sexy!

"First the jacket," she said, feeling as if she'd whispered into his ears and now waited for her words to be heard and obeyed. Making a slight adjustment to the zoom, she watched those long, blunt fingers work on the buttons one by one until he finished and eased off the navy jacket.

"The tie." He worked this off slowly, moving around the elegant modern furniture to turn the television on. A final tug had the silver cloth slipping over his shoulders and into his hands.

"The shirt," she said, realizing her voice was suddenly filled with anticipation. She almost growled when he settled his large arms across his chest and focused on whatever the television was showing.

"Come on, now…the shirt…" After a long pause, he undid his belt buckle and tugged out his white shirt, making him look even sexier.

As a breath of longing clogged her throat, the phone suddenly shrilled, rupturing the anticipation and causing her to jump.

"Damn!" Lowering the binoculars, she snatched up the phone. "What?"

"Is that any way to answer you phone?" the voice on the line reprimanded.

"Oh, hi Mom. Sorry, I thought you were someone else," she lied, but it still got her a short lecture on manners, only to stop abruptly with "Were you expecting a man to call, dear?" In Sharonda's experience that translated into several questions ranging from marriage to grandkids.

"No, Momma."

The rest of the phone conversation was practically identical to the one she'd had with her mother a few days before. By the time she hung up, she knew she'd require an aspirin and decided that from now on, she'd let the answering machine screen her calls.

Once more, she raised the binoculars to search for the man, but frowned in disappointment when she found his curtain closed.

If her mother knew that James Cooper, her childhood friend, was in the apartment across the way, the matchmaking would be in full swing. After the disastrous blind date with James almost a decade ago, she had no burning urge to repeat history. She'd been acutely attracted to him then, but nothing had come of it. It seemed futile to go through the trouble again.

But there was no crime in looking, was there?

James Cooper changed from his work clothes into his oldest jeans and second-best T-shirt. His grandfather owned the apartment complex, and when he'd been offered the apartment; he'd been reluctant to take it. First, because he already had a perfectly good one in a high rise downtown in the heart of corporate San Diego, and second, because taking the apartment would mean that he'd have to play Mr. Fix-it for his favorite grandfather.

Family loyalty won out, so here he was, on his way to the lobby where grandpa had informed him that the soda machine had stopped working. When he pulled the unit away from the wall for closer inspection, he spotted the frayed edge of a burgundy book amid the dust bunnies. It sat like an exposed treasure and for a moment, James had hesitated before reaching for it.

With a good puff, he blew away most of the dust, then wiped at the rest. The words Personal Journal were embossed on the front in curling calligraphy. Seconds of indecision passed as he ran his thumb over the edge of the pages, wanting to nudge in between and take a peek at what was written there. He settled for looking inside the front cover and found S. Williams written in a distinctly feminine hand.

Williams... Williams... Sharonda Williams? Yeah, it had to be her, the latest tenant renting the 7B apartment. As his grandfather had pointed out, it was the same Sharonda from his youth. He hoped the meddlesome old man wasn't matchmaking. Why, it had been about ten years since that awful blind date...

And recently, when he'd seen Sharonda Williams entering the elevator, she'd been wearing conservative gray clothes, flat-heeled shoes and minimal make-up. Although she'd smiled politely, she'd kept her well-rounded size twelve body stiff and distanced from him. At the time, she'd looked familiar, but all he could think was that it was a shame to hide such a luscious ripe body beneath such plain attire.

She'd grown a couple of inches since the high school, lost her thick glasses and was minus the braces. Now she stood five-foot-seven, had shoulder-length black hair and a smooth mahogany brown complexion.

What would a woman like that write in her diary?

The longer he stared at the book, the more he wanted to know. Maybe it was the light scent of floral perfume that had wafted up when he opened the book. Maybe it was the worn spine of the thick book that indicated how often it had been used. Maybe it was the utter temptation to read a woman's most intimate thoughts. A quick flip of the pages revealed a feminine cursive executed by a fine-tipped pen instead of a ball-point. The simple arch of script was utterly tantalizing.

He shut the book quickly, forcing back temptation. After rationalizing that it was too late in the day to return the diary, he took it to his apartment and placed it on the entry table.

When a bad case of insomnia kept him up until three o'clock in the morning, his thoughts wandered back to that blind date years ago.

It had been a church-sponsored fiasco, a thinly-veiled ploy hatched by overprotective mothers to keep their teenage children with others they considered God-fearing and moral. Little did they know that their kids were pre-pubescently horny and desperate for any experience.

The most vivid part of the memory was not the burger they'd shared with another couple, but the keenly embarrassing tension when they'd sat in the front seat listening to the other couple making out in the back seat.

Sure, there had been attraction between them, but hell, he'd been a virgin, too self-conscious to even hold her hand.

At the end of that long horrible night, it had been a relief to go their separate ways. Until now.

Well, he was definitely not a virgin any more, and she was no longer a little girl.

The burning question was, what kind of woman was she?

The question compelled him to arise and go to the entry table where the book lay. The answer seemed to burn through the book when his finger touched the cover. It was then, that without much compunction, he settled onto his sofa, opened the first perfume-teasing page and found himself drowning in the waters of her nightly thoughts.

The words lured him with the strength of yearning found in a poignant phrase; in the way the writing tilted and became less tidy wherever fantasies evolved. The words tied him up in scarf-soft knots as he followed the rawness in her longing.

He read some sentences twice, others three times, then paused to contemplate the ways he could fulfill her wishes. There were comments that begged for tangible experimentation, for carnal discovery.

"I wonder if there's any way to have an orgasm simply by a

man's lips on my breasts or by his tongue licking my ankles... anything but the plain old vanilla intercourse. Harry promised me the world to get the goods, then didn't deliver. Like that was a surprise. Now that I think of it, he was always changing my plans to suit himself. Well, I want my own agenda for a change!"

And what would that self-satisfying agenda be?

James felt his testicles hug tighter to his body; his penis, already half-erect, began to stiffen and elongate in his boxer shorts. He licked his lips and felt the hunger grow.

"Through the binoculars, I've seen the couple in the apartment down the way go at it for about seven minutes. Is there a man alive who can drag out sex for more than ten minutes? And if he's not going to give me an orgasm, at least he ought to give me a good time! A very good time. But every woman deserves an orgasm, doesn't she?"

Yes, he thought, eagerness starting to strain within him. Absolutely. Pages swept past as he lost track of time.

"I wish Harry would ask me what I want. He won't even let me guide his hands to my breasts and when I say something, he looks at me like I'm out of my mind. I'd rather be alone than go through this shit again."

Why hadn't her lover delighted in finding her erogenous zones? He momentarily stared blankly at the page, his mind already busy imagining her naked body and the places he'd willingly explore.

Yes, definitely for more than ten minutes.

He'd make her tell him where she wanted to be touched... how much... and for how long...

His erection twitched, the arousal becoming painful. He turned and read a few more pages.

"Three men in five years and so far, they haven't deviated from the missionary position or the doggie style. I know I'm not petite, but come on! I'm flexible."

James smiled at that.

"So why do I still obsess about sex?"

He read that sentence until the curls and lifts of her handwriting became an elaborate pattern tattooed in his mind. His wristwatch, sitting on the coffee table, beeped the hour, and he wearily rubbed his hand over his face, resisting the urge to rub his hard on and find his relief.

When he turned his attention back to the open book, he ran his fingers slowly over the edge, feeling like a sorcerer with a new book of spells. The frustration between the pages taunted him. His wayward thoughts suddenly dared to find a new purpose. Should he do it? Would he volunteer to give the voluptuous Miss Sharonda Williams the sensual and sexual pleasure she sought? How would he make the offer without seeming like a lecherous psychopath? He read on.

"Okay, so maybe I drank too much tonite, but hellllll. I can see the moon outside my window, and the night is like a mouth, wide open, about to swallow it whole. I wish I could be devoured and ravished like that. Yes, that corny old-fashioned word, "ravished" when I really mean fucked! Except I also mean ravished. Fravished. Done. Well-done and thank you very much.

I want to feel lightning that makes my toes curl with an orgasm, until I don't have to fake anything, until I have to beg whoever it is to stop. From now on, I swear I won't spend another second on Mr. Wrong. Mr. Cheater. Mr. What-the-Hell. It may take the rest of my life, but I'm never going to settle for being fucked by some small-dicked, bad-breath dumb-ass loser ever again."

Everywhere he looked, he saw the words standing out like a code.

I need... I want... I crave... I wish...

Carefully, James marked the page and closed the book, his other hand resting on his erection. If only he could... Would she allow him to...

The soft fragrance of flowers lingered in the air while his questions flourished without answers.

Chapter 2

Even though it hadn't been long since Sharonda had moved in, she'd learned that it was quicker to take the stairs than to bother with the elevator.

So, despite the tightness of the new shoes and the weariness in her bones, she climbed the stairs to her apartment.

The large basket sitting on her doorstep was a surprise and she glanced up and down the hall before picking it up. Sure enough, there was a card with her name printed on it. She peered inside the crinkly, translucent wrapping, finding a bouquet of her favorite peach-colored roses, a bottle of expensive cognac, a small pink votive candles and... her diary!

With shaky fingers, she unlocked her apartment and after checking the hallway, stepped inside, turning on the lights. She placed the vine basket on the kitchen table along with her purse and keys, then after a steadying breath, began to remove the items inside.

Only then did she notice the gift-wrapped box beneath it all. The paper was covered with golden moons and silver stars on a backdrop of navy blue sky. After taking a deep breath, her finger slipped under the tape, carefully, so as not to tear, as she revealed the box. Inside it, she found a beautifully crafted wind chime set. The center was a ceramic iridescent moon while around it stars glimmered like silver coins.

The small note nested at the bottom. "For every moon there must be a sky. Shall I be that sky?" The signature was clearly visible. James Cooper. With his phone number underneath.

Oh my God!!! Holy Heck! Cooper! As in Jimmy Cooper from high school? As in Mr. Sexy from across the way!

She took a deep breath, then released it as she ran her fingers through her hair. After the initial shock passed, she touched the ceramic stars, listening to their gentle round chimes as they touched the moon. Her heart thundered in a mixture of excitement and fear. Her fingers caressed the loved diary she'd thought never to see again. Oh, God, he'd probably read everything!

James Cooper had not apologized for reading her diary. He hadn't even attempted to be anonymous. He'd just written the simple, heart-stopping comment about wanting to be her sky...

She forced her fingers to move, to repack the gift and shoved the whole thing to the corner of the table. Grasping for normalcy, she went into her kitchen and began making a salad for dinner because it was something to do other than hyperventilate.

"Ohhhh Lord," she muttered as she worked.

But the meal proved to be a weak diversion. As she pushed a cherry tomato around, she toyed with the urge to call the bold Mr. Cooper and give him a piece of her mind. Man, she could let him know that it was wrong to... To what? To say he wanted to be her sky? To want to seduce her? Could this remotely be some form of mockery because of the stupid childhood date?

Anxiety and anger fueled her as she reached into the basket for his number and then grabbed the phone to dial.

On the second ring, the phone was picked up, and James's smooth, deep voice answered. "Hello?"

All emotion fizzled and she gripped the receiver, trying to find the words that had deserted her. When the pause became embarrassing and tense, she started to hang up the phone, but paused when she heard, "Sharonda?"

He said her name softly, with the quiet hush of calm ocean waves settling upon a beach. "Don't hang up."

She inhaled sharply, the air clearing her head enough for the anger to form. "You had no right! Those were my most personal thoughts and now you dare to exploit them?"

"I'm sorry—"

"No, you're not—"

He paused. "You're partially right. I'm not sorry I read the diary. I'm just sorry I've obviously frightened you."

She gripped the phone hard. "Do you even remember me?"

"You mean, do I remember the blind date from back in high school?"

Damn, he remembered! "I know your grandfather, you know? I'd bet he'd be interested in what a little pervert his grandson is."

To her surprise, the rumble of James' chuckle sounded mischievous and unembarrassed. "How do you know I'm not a pervert by heredity? Come on. If I was a pervert, I would've mauled you on our blind date ages ago."

The words worked, the bit of humor bringing a twitch to her lips. Relief eased the tension in her shoulders. "Well—"

"Look." His voice sobered a bit. "I couldn't resist the temptation to read your diary. Okay, I was wrong. Maybe unforgivably wrong. But your fantasies were irresistible... You have so many questions that I think I know how to answer... "

Sharonda closed her eyes, mesmerized by the promise in the tone of his voice. She swallowed but didn't reply. In the silence, a shift of sound revealed his brief movement.

Straightening her spine, she drew in a breath, determined to break the spell. "Thanks, but this macho quest—"

"You know it's not that."

"What is it then?"

He paused dramatically. "I've given it a lot of thought, so I don't want you to take what I say lightly... You wrote that you dream of a stranger, yet someone familiar. I fit both categories —"

"God, I can't believe it—!"

"I know, I know." A brief silence followed the statement. Then he sighed and continued. "Sharonda, think about it. Really think about it. I'm humbly and respectfully proposing an opportunity for us to experiment with your fantasies."

She gasped, her mind literarily going blank for a moment before she found her voice, weak as it was. "I can't believe what I just heard you say."

"Be honest with me for a minute." He sounded like a professional negotiator, convincing. Yet that undertone of husky persuasion filtered through. "You've obviously wondered what it would be like to have someone to play out your fantasies with."

"James, you don't even know me anymore! I'm not the girl I once was. I don't know you!" she whispered, the yearning in her voice making the argument sound weak.

"Take a chance on me."

"I can't. I'm not like that."

He sighed. "Sharonda, I'll bet a hundred bucks you have binoculars you use—"

"So what?" she snapped defensively.

"Wouldn't you like to just try what you wrote on page thirty-two? It's simple and harmless. And you have the ultimate control. All you have to do is hang the wind chimes outside and I'll know you want me to call on you."

15

Page thirty-two? Hang the wind chimes? What? "You're crazy."

"The wind chimes will be our calling card. If I don't see it, I'll forget the whole thing. If I do… I'll come over. It's up to you."

She gasped and abruptly hung up the phone. Then in a rush, she ran for the binoculars, dimmed the lights and peered out the parted curtain to the distant apartment.

James, handsome as always, was placing the phone back on the cradle. As he straightened, he single-handedly loosened his tie, then used both hands to undo the buttons of his shirt. It was then that she noticed he was still looking in her general direction, a sexy, mischievous smile on his lips, as if to let her know that he knew she was watching him.

In a huff, she turned away, pulled the curtain shut and sank onto the couch. It was almost ten whole minutes later when she finally gave in and grabbed her diary, noticing how he had numbered the pages at the bottom.

"Bastard!" she muttered, only half meaning it.

Page thirty-two trembled under her fingertips as she read her own handwriting.

"For once I'd like it to be about me. No sex, just me, masturbating. Just like my sweet dream last night. I'd touch myself and get off while a stranger watches, or stimulates me, wanting me but unable to have me."

Chapter 3

For a whole week, Sharonda pretended she'd never received the vine basket that adorned the middle of her kitchen table. So what if she peered at him on occasion through her binoculars? It was simple curiosity.

The temptation of the wind chimes tormented her thoughts. Would he do anything she asked? Any sexual thrill at all? Was his perception of her that she was desperate or that she was easy or what?

Sharonda parked her car and stepped out into the surly weather. October in San Diego was strange. Sometimes, blazing hot, sometimes downright cold. Today was a cool, breezy day.

Since she felt bone weary from working overtime, she decided to take the elevator rather than the stairs.

The old elevator doors had almost slid shut when a hand pushed hard enough for the doors to reluctantly swing open.

"Hold the elevator, please. I—" James Cooper stepped into the small space, looking as surprised to see her as she was to see him. The sentence dangled unfinished while she stared at him.

His gaze held hers and the silence was disturbed by the muffled thump of the closing door and the ancient gears engaging to pull the elevator upward. Sharonda gripped her purse tightly and tried to control the odd thrill that snaked down her spine.

Up close, he was even more handsome than what the binoculars revealed. He looked impeccably clean, his clothes meticulous and neat, and he smelled lightly of a citrus cologne. His wire-rimmed glasses gave him an intellectual air, but it was the seductive heat of his gaze that stole her breath.

She licked her lips nervously, and felt another thrill when his eyes traced the movement. His nostrils flared and his full lips moved slightly.

"Beautiful weather, isn't it?" he asked, his voice husky in the silence.

She glanced at his tie, his shoes, his chin. What had he said? The weather? "Yeah. It's nice." Damn, but he was handsome.

Too bad he'd read her diary! Or was it?

He eased one hand over his tie and slipped it into the pocket of his trousers. "Supposed to be a full moon tonight."

Oh, Lord! "Really?" A sudden hunger for him watered in her mouth.

Yes." His eyes let her know he was also remembering. ...the night is like a mouth, wide open, about to swallow it whole...

The elevator door opened but Sharonda felt lost in the depths of his hazel brown eyes. When the door began to close again, he reached out and held it, his eyes still locked with hers.

"Sweet dreams," he finally said before exiting the elevator.

The sexy hazy feeling remained all the way to her apartment, becoming seeds of temptation. Under the spray of a soothing shower, she could hear his words again, like pillow talk… "Sweet dreams".

Sharonda slipped into her purple robe with nothing under but a pair of black panties, letting the silk of the robe caress her breasts, her thighs, her skin. She lit the freesia-scented candles and let their soft glow build an ambience in the room. Tonight seemed like a perfect night to be swallowed whole.

The bottle of cognac was opened not because of him, she firmly told herself, but because she deserved it. After filling her wineglass with the amber liquid and curling up on the couch, she looked through the other contents of the vine basket and debated what to do while sipping the decadent liquor. The worlds between her fantasies and reality were about to merge if she took this step. Or was that when rather than if?

Frustrated, she turned on the TV, but found nothing interesting to her. With an exasperated flick of her thumb, she pressed the remote and turned it off.

The TV screen was a fuzzy reflection as she stared blindly at it, toying with a strand of curly hair, weighing the decision she was about to make. The second glass of the amber liquid warmed her even more. The candles smelled fantastic and like a tide, she felt her needs creeping closer to the deciding edge.

One glance outside proved that true to his prediction, a full moon crested the nocturnal sky, presenting itself to the night. Pale moonlight filtered in, picking up the iridescent gleam of the wind chimes in the open box, and Sharonda found herself reaching for it.

This was James she was thinking of! Not the teenage boy that had sat mortified next to her in the car on their horrific date. This was a man, the man she lusted over, the man who could stall her mind with a single look.

This man knew exactly what she wanted. And did she ever want it.

Twice she second-guessed herself, standing up to head for the balcony, only to sit down again. Finally, she worked up the nerve to take the chime outside, unhooking one of her hanging plants, and replacing it with the gift. The breeze immediately stirred the chimes, as if releasing a spell.

Across the pool, the curtain moved in James' apartment, and she saw his silhouette watching her. Despite the wine, Sharonda felt instantly sober, frozen in place for what felt like an eternity.

The wind pushed her hair into her face and tugged at the robe. Tucking her hair behind her ear, she turned away from him and hurried inside. No sooner had the sliding door closed than she heard the phone ring. Once. Twice. She snatched it on the third ring.

For a few seconds, she heard nothing but the muffled sound of the wind chimes.

"You put the chimes out," he said, as casually as he'd mentioned the full moon earlier.

At long last, she replied a bit breathlessly, "I—I— Don't say anything, okay? Just let me do it."

"No." The single words sounded deeper than she remembered, gruffer.

"No?"

"You are always brave in your fantasies. Be brave now. Let it be just like your dreams."

She turned toward the open drapes that allowed him to look into her apartment. Even without her binoculars, she could see him watching her.

"Yes, let me watch," he coaxed. "You know you want me to."

"I can't believe I'm doing this..."

He paused. "You don't have to do anything you don't want to. Do you want to call it off?"

Her own hesitation spoke volumes. Her whispered reply even more. "No."

He exhaled, as if he'd been unsure of the outcome. "Then... show me what it was that you were dreaming of."

She sank onto the comfortable couch, feeling the silk robe caress her body as it rearranged itself around her. Despite the dividing distance, she could feel his gaze on her, everywhere.

"Don't be nervous. Relax. Lean your head back and relax. This is your fantasy... live it."

The cognac and the hint of passion in his voice firmed her resolve. Without his saying another word, she shifted her hips and began to slide her panties down.

"Beautiful," he murmured, his voice becoming thick with appreciation. "You have very sexy legs... Very sexy..."

She undid the tie of her purple robe, letting gravity tug the edges ever so slightly apart. Her breasts remained hidden, but the robe revealed her belly button and the entire length of her legs.

His breathing changed, becoming rougher. Sharonda felt like smiling at the sudden sensual power she commanded. "You are a pervert."

"So, torture me," he challenged.

She shifted slightly and the robe opened a bit wider. "Like that?"

"Spread your thighs a bit more... More... Yes... Better yet, place your left leg on the armrest."

She obeyed. For almost a full minute, all she could hear was the reckless beating of her heart and the slow, controlled rhythm of his aroused breathing. The headiness was more than cognac, more than any foreplay in the past.

"Touch yourself," he whispered.

It seemed surreal already, with him whispering over the phone, her head leaning back. Yet, she was incredibly aroused, knowing she was living out one of her most private fantasies.

Feeling wanton, she moved her hand slowly over her belly, her thighs, her pubic hair, until her fingers were touching her clitoris. With personal familiarity, she moved her fingers over the sensitive nub, over to the swollen lips of labia, closing her eyes to feel the trace of her finger pads.

She dipped her fingers into the wet folds of her sex and stroked the wetness upward, swirling it over her clitoris.

"Yes." His breathless voice sounded as if he was lurking in the nearby shadows. "Again."

She complied, licking her dry lips and fondling the swollen labia until her fingers were knuckle-deep inside the wet, moist passage. Moments passed without words, just the sound of uneven breathing, low modes of approval and the quiet slick noises of her wet fingers as they played into her vagina.

"Fuck." He uttered the word like a sacred exclamation, involuntarily, but she decided to take it as a request and began to move her fingers in a plunge-and-withdrawing tempo that matched the churn of her hips.

"Oh," she groaned, her mind absorbed in the single task of masturbation. She moved a hand over the robe to her breast, caressing and squeezing the tight nipple, the phone barely nestling between the couch and her ear.

Her panting grew, her occasional moans becoming louder with the rush of pleasure.

"Put the phone closer to your fingers," James said into her ear, his voice filled with sexual urgency. "I want to hear more..."

She slipped the phone down until it was as close to her fingers as possible.

Deliberately, she began to harden the motion of her thrusts, pushing, rubbing and stroking the juicy-slick labia and clitoris with her arousal. The phone trembled in her hand as the pleasure built to the point where she could hardly stand it.

"Oh! Oh! Umh!" She cried out, arching her back and bucking her hips into her hand. "J-James..." The tremors rolled over her in waves, until at last she lay limp and satisfied, feeling the final ripples of ecstasy on her fingers.

Belatedly, she realized that the phone still nested on her inner thigh. Several seconds passed before she picked it up and brought it to her ear, too exhausted to feel embarrassed or prudish.

"Thank you," James said, breathing hard. By the tone of his voice, she judged he hadn't found his own release. "That was absolutely, unbelievably, beautiful."

"Can I watch you?" she blurted before common sense

intervened. She opened her eyes and stared at the unclear picture of him across the distance to his apartment.

"Yes," he said without any hesitation whatsoever.

Feeling the first signs of renewed energy, she wiped her fingers, then reached for the binoculars and focused them into his apartment. A lamp haloed him with soft light where he sat on his couch. His binoculars were trained on her, but they lowered and he slowly rested his head back, the phone by his ear.

He'd removed his jacket, but he was still wearing his stark white shirt and black trousers. The shirt had been unbuttoned, the tie skewed and the zipper of his trousers was undone. His long, thick, black erection thrust upward in his solid grip. At the base of his thick stalk, his testicles looked bulbous and tight.

"Hmmm, yes," she murmured as he watched his hand stroke his length with a familiar touch, the soft hushed sounds of his shirt marking the movements.

With eyes shut, he spoke into the phone. "Are you watching?"

Hell yes! "Nice grip. Impressive."

His panting was getting harder, his strokes becoming faster.

"Did you masturbate when you read my diary?" she whispered.

He licked his lips, the sound becoming intimate over the

phone. "Yes."

Sharonda could see the pre-cum gleaming at the tip of his penis and she swallowed, wondering if she'd truly ever admired a penis before.

"You're so thick," she admitted, hearing his groan as he worked his long-fingered hand over his cock, back and forth, back and forth. "And long."

His reply was more of a hiss as he stroked himself twice more, barely holding back the shudder that sent his white ejaculation squirting in the air, landing mostly on his tie.

His grunts sounded like half-bitten words. When his hand finally rested, he breathed a tremulous sigh. She felt it clear over the phone wires.

He lifted his head, a small smile playing on his lips.

"Thank you," she whispered.

"You're welcome."

There was a comfortable silence to the aftermath, but she kept her eyes trained on him, delighting in the way his fingers still trailed gently over his penis.

When he spoke again, his voice was filled with polite curiosity. "Have you ever masturbated for anyone before?"

"No. You?"

"No."

She focused the lens on the stains on his tie and the way his ejaculation had formed such an interesting pattern. Silence followed. "I, ah, I guess I should put the wind chimes back inside."

"Okay... Sharonda?"

"Yes?"

"Next time, how about page fifty-nine?"

"Fifty-nine?" What had she written? "We'll see," was all she said, crossing her legs and shielding her body with the robe.

"Okay."

"Okay."

A long pause followed but when she heard Mrs. Benson letting her cat out, Sharonda stood and closed the balcony curtain. She was certain the elderly woman couldn't see her, but she wanted to hold on to this moment for just a while more. She'd let the wind chimes sing a little longer before bringing them inside.

"Good night," she said, still somewhat unwilling to disconnect.

"Thanks to you, it certainly is..."

With a wistful sigh, she hung up the phone.

Chapter 4

Later that night, Sharonda lay on the soft bedspread, a kiwi cucumber facemask caking from neglect, a towel wrapped turban style on her head. Because her blood drummed with anticipation, she'd deliberately waited until she could no longer stand it, then pulled out her diary and flipped to page fifty-nine.

I wonder if there's any way to have an orgasm simply by a man's lips on my breasts or by his tongue, licking my ankles...anything but the plain old vanilla intercourse.

"I see," she muttered, feeling a faint blush of embarrassment. He wanted to give her an orgasm, knowing that she wanted to avoid intercourse.

Well, he was definitely a virile and able man that much was obvious. Maybe he thought he was going to get lucky in the process.

For crying out loud, she knew nothing about him! It wasn't that she didn't trust him. Not entirely. But still, they had shared something deeply personal.

The facial tingled as she studied the ceiling. If she decided to allow him to do page fifty-nine (and that was a big if), things had to be on her terms.

She wrestled with the idea even after she'd washed off the facial and finished smearing lotion on her face. She finished plucking her eyebrows, which brought another thought to mind; a pubic wax job. And a pedicure wouldn't be a bad idea either. And if she took a long, Freesia-scented bath beforehand…

"Damn," she said, frowning at herself in the mirror, realizing that somewhere in her subconscious, she'd already decided she was going to hang the chimes again after all.

A long sigh later, she pulled the towel off her head. Isn't this what she'd always dreamed of? Her belly filled with butterfly tremors, some from anxiety, some from anticipation. The smile reflecting in the mirror seemed like a combination of the two. James Cooper might be just the kind of fling she needed.

Ten years had changed her completely. And they had certainly changed him too.

Well, since she was going to go through with this, she'd have to take care of the grooming first.

It took two days to complete the beautification process, and in the meantime, her sexual suspense was mounting. When it became obvious that James planned on keeping his

29

curtain half-way open, Sharonda began doing the same, heeding the unspoken invitation to share glimpses into their lives.

That evening, it took her a bit by surprise to peer through the binoculars at James' apartment and find him looking right back at her, wearing nothing but a white T-shirt and green boxer shorts, binoculars in hand. From where he sat on the couch, he'd probably been there a while.

She'd hesitated before waving.

He'd smiled, slow and knowing, then briefly waved back.

He looked positively edible! Feeling suddenly nervous, she tried to hide the wind chimes behind her back as she stepped out of view. When the phone rang a few seconds later, she knew he must have seen it.

"Hello?" She put down the binoculars and tugged at her purple robe, remembering the last time she wore it for him.

"Changing your mind?" he asked, his voice sounding sensual and quiet.

"Well, no. Not exactly. I, ah, I think I need just a bit more time."

"Ah." He made that sound amazingly neutral.

"I wasn't really going to hang it up right now," she hedged, feeling the need to ramble. "I was just..."

"Just?"

"Just thinking about it."

Silence filled the gap like a long first kiss. "That's good."

Sharonda studied the seam of her robe, tracing the edge

with her finger, mentally phrasing and re-phrasing her words before pushing them from her lips. "Would tomorrow be good?" Hell, sound fast and easy, why don't you, she reprimanded herself.

To his credit, he didn't mock her at how quick it had taken her to 'think about it.' But when he did reply, the timbre of his voice sent a familiar warm shiver down her spine. "What time?"

"Um, about eight?"

"I have clients from out of town, so just to be safe, how about nine?"

"Alright." She nibbled her bottom lip, fighting down a sudden need to laugh. Goodness, but he made her feel bold!

"What's so funny?" he asked curiously, and she realized he was still watching her.

"It's just that this sounds so… formal."

He chuckled. "Should I ask if it's a suit and tie occasion."

She grinned, relaxing a bit. "Were you planning on wearing a suit?"

"Unless you prefer the whips and chains," he said, his voice full of humor.

She laughed. "How about we start off with something a little tamer."

"Like a business suit?"

"Yeah." Her words came out hungrier, breathier than she'd intended. He had no idea how she lusted after him in a suit.

"I'm game. Which one would you like?"

Grabbing her binoculars, she looked over at him. "The one you had on yesterday."

"Yesterday?"

Or the day before, or the one you had on earlier. You wear them all so well. "Yes."

"White shirt?"

"Mmm-hmm."

"Black trousers?"

"Mmm-hmm."

"What tie?"

"Do you have a navy blue one?" she asked, knowing he did.

"Yes. Anything else?"

"Leave the jacket behind."

His sensual grin flashed. "Then I guess that means I can make some requests of my own, right?"

"That depends," she said, flashing him a smile.

"On?"

"Your kink factor."

His voice rumbled with brief laughter. "Shucks. I suppose that it being the first time and all, I'll tone down my request."

"You're such a gentleman."

"I try."

Her mind held on to those words like a promise. "Okay, let me have your list."

She could see his index finger adjusting the zoom of his binoculars. "High heels. With four to six inches."

"Don't think I have any."

"Really?"

Why did she have the sneaky suspicion that he was sure she didn't. "But I'll find a pair. Anything else?"

His voice sounded smoky. "Absolutely. Black nylons. Thigh-high."

She nodded, feeling her breath start to hitch. "No whipped cream or chocolate-dipped strawberries?"

He paused for a moment. "Damn tempting... but if I bring anything it'll be a surprise."

Like what? Apprehension billowed. "Normally, I don't mind surprises, but—"

"But by the way you're nibbling on your lip, you don't want any now, right?"

"Right." A slight pause followed and she lowered her binoculars.

"I get the feeling this isn't about strawberries," he said. "What's on your mind?"

She shrugged. "This is all very strange, don't you think? I know next to nothing about you and yet here I am..."

"Taking a chance on an erotic escapade."

She nodded.

"For what it's worth, I've never done this sort of thing before. I mean, I'm taking a chance too."

How so? She wanted to ask.

"Are you worried about protection?" His concern sounded genuine.

"That's part of it."

"Let's see. I use condoms and I've never had a sexually transmitted disease... And by your diary, I know you're STD-free and on birth control pills, right?"

Sharonda felt suddenly vulnerable. "Right. See what I mean? You know too much about me. I should've asked questions before, but—"

"But we both had other things on our minds."

"Yes."

His voice warmed. "What do you remember about me from ten years ago? We were in the choir together. We had the same type of meddlesome moms. We had an unforgettable blind date. If you want to know more, ask me anything."

There were so many questions that jockeyed to be asked.

"Are you seeing anyone?"

"No."

"Come on now. A man like you?"

He paused, his voice carrying a trace of humor. "Should I be offended by that?"

"You know what I mean."

"For the record, Sharonda, I'm single. Not dating, seeing or interested in being with anyone but you."

It seemed too good to be true! "Oh." Did he have any idea

what his words were doing to her?

"I'm not a player, Sharonda. I like exclusivity."

Lord knows she couldn't take another cheating lover. "Me too."

The minute she said the words, she knew that he'd read her diary and knew all about it. Embarrassment crept into her cheeks. What were the odds that he was emotionally playing her like a puppet? Well, this wasn't serious anyway. She couldn't let her heart get into it.

Deciding to change the topic, she asked, "What do you do for a living?"

The conversation started slowly and comfortably as he explained his job as an architect. One subject led to another until she relaxed into her chair, listening to him explain his passion for a cappella singers, his love for mountain hiking, and his obsession with gadgets. When Sharonda checked the clock, she was surprised to see that they had been talking for about two hours.

When conversation dwindled into a cozy silence, she raised the binoculars in time to see him touch his ear lobe in an unusually fidgety gesture. "I saw a silk negligee at Victoria's Secret, the same color as your robe. Would you let me buy it for you?"

She'd been expecting a change of subject, yet the request caught her by surprise. "You don't have to do that."

He lowered the binoculars and she studied the graceful,

honest lines of his face, hearing him say, "I really want to."

She hesitated.

"Look, I understand that tomorrow isn't about sex between us. It's all about you. But I just want to give you this one gift."

She was startled that he planned on honoring her fantasy to that degree. "Alright."

"Thank you. I'll have it delivered to you."

"But you don't know my measurements."

"Oh, I think I can make an accurate guess."

Sharonda didn't know whether to be insulted or pleased. She settled for pleased. "If you say so."

"Trust me."

Ah, yes. Two simple yet complicated words. Smiling, she said, "Okay."

The next morning, Sharonda called in sick to work and spent the morning cleaning up her apartment, then spent the afternoon shopping for the perfect pair of high heels, because, as James had suspected, she didn't own a single pair. Once in the store, deciding was pure torture. Would he like the feather boa ones that her friend often referred to as "fuck-me pumps"? Or did he prefer the classic elegance of single-strapped high heels. Ah, and then there was satin! Was that preferable to leather shoes? And how could she possibly go to the register with those shoes in her hand?

There were too many beautiful shoes to decide, so she bought several pairs, including peek-a-boo toe tips that showed off her red nail-polish and five-inch red Italian stilettos that screamed sex.

Only when she caught a glimpse of her goofy smile did she realize how wickedly bold she felt. Anticipation made her also feel sexy. Hoisting the bag of shoes, she hurried to her car.

Back in her apartment, she fussed with her hair, retouched her makeup and rubbed a subtle lotion all over her body.

When the doorbell rang announcing her surprise gift, she was on pins and needles. She hurried to answer the door, trying to hide the flash of surprise when she found Mr. Cooper leaning on his cane, a package balanced in his hand.

"Hey, there, young lady," he greeted her, eyes twinkling.

"Hello, Mr. Cooper!"

"Special delivery. The courier didn't say from where, but anyone can see you got yourself an admirer."

She reached for the lovely gift-wrapped package. "It might just be my sister, sending me a late birthday gift," she lied.

"That so?" the wizened man asked with a disbelieving gleam in his bespeckled eyes. He was a short, stout man with full head of white hair and a moustache to match.

Ever since she could remember, he'd looked the same, like

37

he belonged in a jazz club among wailing brass and slow-rising smoke. Instead, he ran the small apartment complex as if every tenant was part of his extended family. "Ain't you supposed to be at work?"

"I wasn't feeling well this morning," she lied, adding a sniff for effect.

"Coming down with something?"

A blazing case of horniness. And boy am I in a bad way! Instead, she calmly said, "Just some minor cold symptoms... you know."

The mention of symptoms sent him off on the subject of his gout and then his arthritis and somehow that led to talk about the weather. As always, their conversation wasn't over until the old man had boasted about his good-hearted grandson, James Cooper, referring to the thirty-year-old man as the 'boy.'

"You should see him fixing things. I mean, when he sets his mind to something, he sure gets the job done! That kind of drive is hard to find these days."

She nodded, wondering where the conversation was headed, saying nothing, since he didn't really require more from her.

"Have you seen him lately? If'n I remember correctly, you knew each other from school or something."

Why did she suddenly suspect her mother's hand was in this? "Um, yeah. Church," she replied.

38

"Had you a date of some sort, right? Talked with your mom a while back and I think she brought it up."

Subtle matchmaking, Mom! "Yeah, it was one of those church functions, I think," Sharonda replied vaguely. "Something like that."

"Did he tell you he's an architect now?"

Sharonda suppressed the urge to sigh, refusing to admit she'd even spoken or met with bachelor number one. "Really?"

"Designed the art center down by the pier, you know, the one with—" The buzz of his pager interrupted him. He mumbled something as he read the small display.

"Well, I've got to go take care of this. You have a nice day and I'll have to catch you later."

"You too, Mr. Cooper. Thanks for the delivery."

She hurriedly closed the door when he shuffled off. Carrying the package to the couch, she began to carefully remove the paper, lifting the lid of the box to uncover the stunning lacy black and lavender creation inside. Amazingly, he'd picked out just the right size. Well, pretty close. At least he'd allowed for enough elasticity for the garment to accommodate her curves.

The demi-cups had little Velcro strips that could peel off to reveal her breasts. The dangling satin and lace garters attached to nylons, but the most daring part of the design was the dark purple iris tucked into the lacy crotchless panties!

That night as James entered his apartment he noticed that Sharonda's curtain was closed, obstructing any view into her apartment. As it was already eight-thirty, and he was running late, he placed the gift bag and the flowers by the entry table and hurried to take a shower, his stomach in anxious turmoil.

Ten minutes later, he was in the designated clothing, straightening his tie in the mirror as if he had a job interview. It was the navy blue tie, since for Sharonda nothing else would do. He chuckled at himself, amazed at how eager he felt, wanting to get over to Sharonda's place. Even after masturbating in the shower, he could feel his body primed, on sexual stand-by.

She'd been on his mind all day. And she'd certainly dominated his nights with not only the image of her curvy body, but also with the passion in her written thoughts. Her words seemed to haunt him from the closed pages of her journal, and in dreams they were spoken by her, in a soft sultry voice that had him waking up to find his body reacting passionately...

Soon he'd be able to match reality to his fantasies... Soon.

Chapter 5

At nine o'clock, on the hour, the doorbell to Sharonda's apartment rang.

The tiny charm moon-and-star in her ankle bracelet made a clinking sound as she walked somewhat unsteadily on high heels to the door. The black fishnets brought a bold awareness to her legs and the purple robe felt as if it hid nothing of the black lace and satin negligee.

Her heart pounded madly in her chest, and her hands twisted a hard bow on the tie of her robe while a thousand doubts assaulted her mind.

She peered through the peephole at him, and felt her anxiety wane when she saw him holding a bouquet of purple irises, looking handsome as hell.

Sharonda opened the door and stared at him for a few seconds, instant chemistry sizzling between them.

"May I come inside?" he asked huskily.

He was there, inches from her. Real. And if she said yes, he would be her dream lover.

"Yes." She opened the door wider and let him in.

If there had been chemistry at the sight of him, the proximity of him left her speechless with the illicit possibilities that sprang to mind.

"You keep looking at me like that and I'm going to get ideas," James teased, his eyes straying to her lips.

The snappy reply she thought of stalled in her mind and she numbly clutched the bouquet of flowers he'd handed her.

"They're beautiful. Thank you," she said, remembering the single iris on her bedside table.

Feeling naked and awkward, she gave the flowers a perfunctory gaze before her eyes strayed back to James. MMmmm-mmmm! The sleeves of his shirt were rolled up to his forearms, revealing strong muscles and hands.

"Sharonda," he warned, and she hurriedly turned, walking to the kitchen for a vase. His low moan didn't escape her ears, and she realized he was checking out the rear view of fishnets and high-heeled shoes.

"So, hard day at work?" she asked, trying to break the expectant silence. The minute the words were out, she heard the nuance. She looked over her shoulder to see if he'd noticed.

"It's been that way lately," he said, completely straight-faced.

Sharonda kept her hands in the cold water as she adjusted the flowers in the vase. Sparks of desire were already spreading in her gut and the cold water was minimal help.

With a paper towel, she wiped the glass down, knowing

she was stalling, yet holding on to the vase as if it were a trophy.

"You're trembling," he said into the following silence, stepping closer. "Don't be afraid. It's just me, James."

"I know." Her hands stayed on the vase.

"I can leave if you like."

She looked at him, startled. "No. I—I'm just...just..."

He touched a strand of hair by her cheek. "I know."

And somehow, she knew that he understood how giddy, eager and nervous she was. It gave her the incentive to reach for his classic navy blue tie just as his hand cupped her neck. She tugged lightly. He leaned closer, lowering his head.

Their lips met.

The effect was like hot coals in cool water, starting a boil that threatened to become steam. His mouth slanted over hers and she parted her lips for the kiss, her moan melting into his groan.

It was as if that was all that ever existed, hot lips, hot breath and an unquenchable thirst for more. His tongue explored, demanded, flirted, flicked and licked with maddening skill. Half a step closer put them into body contact, and her hand abandoned his tie to reach around his neck. His hands felt like they were everywhere, roaming over her hips, her waist, and, damn him, just short of touching her breasts. Why didn't he just open the robe?!

"James..." she pleaded when they broke apart to gasp for

breath.

He answered with another kiss that made her so breathless she felt dizzy. And still their mouths drank and drank of each other, tasting as if the flavors were forbidden, lusting as if the moment would be gone.

His large hands curved over her buttocks, squeezing and molding her hips against his obvious erection, rocking gently.

She could hardly do anything more than cling to him when his mouth moved to her cheek, then her jaw, then to suck ever so intimately on the pulse at her neck.

"Oh, Jesus," she whimpered.

His teeth nipped gently, taunting. "Now-now," he admonished breathily. "What's a church-going woman like you doing by taking the Lord's name in vain? Hmmm?"

He didn't give her a chance to respond as he lifted her in his strong arms, seating her on the counter while his mouth found hers again.

The kiss slowed and with a final flick of his tongue to her bottom lip, he stepped back. "Beautiful."

She felt it. She'd never felt beautiful in this sense before. But here in her kitchen with a man who was practically a stranger staring lustfully at her, she felt gorgeous.

She noticed that James was careful not to touch her when he pushed the vase to a safe distance down the counter top, as if he was trying to regain control. He then stood in front of her, leisurely removing his silk tie.

In his trousers, his hard-on was seriously shoving against the zipper, but his controlled features told her he had a plan. Even the harsh kitchen light was kind to his handsome face. His eyes were the most seductive hues of dark forest bark. His lips were full and male and looked very, very tempting. His perfect nose flared at the nostrils, and she could hear him as he inhaled.

In his hand, his tie was rolled in a careful motion, hand over hand, until it formed an odd lumpy shape. He cradled it in his palm, his lips forming a boyish smile. He eyed where the black fishnets disappeared beneath the lilac robe, then reached for the tie of the robe, and with his eyes locked on hers, he tugged slowly.

Like a spent breath, the silk unraveled with a hushed sound, allowing the garment to part like water. He looked down where her body was revealed, displaying the full lush line of her cleavage wrapped in the lacy negligee he'd given her. He viewed the abundance of bronze-brown skin, pausing at where the tight iris-black nipples strained the cups. The dark purple silk intertwined with the clever placement of black lace was more than he had dreamed.

Only when he finally tugged the robe from her shoulders did he speak, his gaze more lustful, appreciative. "I know I said it, but... damn, you're beautiful... You've got the kind of curves men dream about, don't you know?"

When he touched her, it was to place her hands against the

counter for support. Then as he straightened, he breathed in the light perfume from the base of her neck.

"Unbutton your shirt," she said, her words sounding rusty as they rushed from her mouth.

Each button that fell from the loop revealed taut black skin fortified by strong muscle. Tonight was supposed to be about her secret fantasies, but she wondered what he'd do if she tossed him on her kitchen floor and had her wicked way with him.

"Open your legs," he said as if he was having the same thoughts she was.

Sharonda shifted against the robe she sat on, parting her thighs for him. The smells of her arousal hung in the air between them and she watched as his eyes slid shut, inhaling quietly, as if mesmerized.

"I want to taste you there," he said, opening his eyes again.

"Now?" She wanted to tell him he could taste her anywhere he wanted!

"Not yet." As if remembering his silk tie, he moved it to the apex of her legs, his knuckles brushing her inner thighs as he lodged the intricate knot of silk hard against her mons.

"It's called a silk dragon," he explained, his wide palms rubbing against the garters from thighs to hips. "Lean forward," he commanded. Sharonda pushed forward until her clitoris was pushing right against a hump of the silk dragon.

"Now, point your toes."

The high heels made it an easy task, bringing about an unexpected shiver that trailed down her spine like a current, catching her by surprise. It shimmered for seconds against her clitoris, leaking her vaginal fluids against his tie.

"Oh!"

With a knowing gleam in his eyes, he crossed her legs at the knees, then grabbed the tie of her robe and made a sensual torture of wrapping it around her knees, even going as far as to make a silly bow.

"Are you comfortable?" he asked.

Well, she was horny, at the edge of something she'd never done and amazed that she never knew just how aroused she could become without doing something about it. Between her legs the silk dragon sat thick and intimate, the two distinctive ridges settled before and after her clitoris.

The slightest motion against it was making her hot all over... in her mouth, her breasts, her nipples, her crotch, even the back of her knees!

"Is that a yes?"

"No."

For the first time, concern overcame the ardor in his eyes.

"I mean. I'm-I'm... fine. Really."

The lazy smile curled on his lips again and he moved closer, his hands settling on her hips to nudge her forward just a bit. "Good."

The movements of her clitoris against the wet dragon

made her bite her lip, to suppress a whimper.

"Yes," he encouraged in a low tone. "Now, point your toes." She closed her eyes and was in the process of doing as he said when he lowered his mouth to her breast, taking the sensitive flesh into his mouth, lace and all. And there he suckled, keeping the nipple in the warmth of his mouth. The sensations tripped over themselves, warm tongue and lips feeling urgent despite the sensual textures of the lace. Every suck became more sensitive, making her breasts feel heavy and swollen.

"Oh, mmm."

What had been a shiver before was now a stronger jolt that connected to the oral tug of his mouth. Emotions were revved, vying for attention. Where his hands slowly rocked her hips against the dragon, she was creamed and squirming. Where his hot tongue suckled again through the lace, the emotion was almost unbearable.

She moaned loudly once and found herself reaching for him, but he put her hands back on the counter where she arched her back to better control the rocking motion. He sucked on her breast and tugged on her hips, back and forth in a rhythmic pace that she adopted.

The first orgasm hit her when he spoke against her breast, reminding her to point her toes. As she did so, he sank a soft bite into her nipple, molding his mouth more firmly on her breast.

"AAAhh!" Her head fell back and she was vaguely aware of the dishes rattling in the cabinet when her head made contact with the wood.

Oh, Lord! He hadn't even moved to the other breast yet, she thought with a sense of wonder.

She could hear his harsh breathing mixing in with hers, but his hands kept up the push-grind motion on her hips, settling her into the two-humped tie, slick with the messy aftermath of her orgasm.

Then he moved to the other breast, teasing it, licking and nuzzling it, tugging her hips into a newer rhythm that put her right back on the edge.

"James... James, please..."

The faint sound of Velcro rippled through her moan, and suddenly the mouth-moistened lacy bra cups were removed.

Her bare breasts were displayed, full and blushed from being so thoroughly kissed. Pushing his shirt open, he pulled her to him, pushing her breasts against his chest, fitting his mouth to hers and giving her a slick hard tug against the humps of the dragon. The knotted tie was lubricated so thoroughly that the action caused it to slip halfway into her, unleashing the second orgasm.

Sharonda felt herself quivering everywhere, from her pointed toes to her sensitive nipples to the tongue-lashing kiss that was robbing her of breath.

She clutched James' shoulders and rode the rest of the

aftershocks while the kiss went on and on…

"James," she pleaded, feeling weak and lightheaded. He whispered something incomprehensible and suddenly gripped her hard, grunting, his breath heavy and jagged in her ear… a lovely sound to his unsteady orgasm.

For several long moments, they simply remained in that position, both of them too weak to move.

When she felt his thumb caressing the rim of her ear, she looked up at him. "Wow."

His smile lingered.

She kissed the moist line of his lips. "Thanks."

One breath followed another. "Oh, we're not done."

Incredible! "Good. Although I hate to tell you this, I think I killed the dragon."

He chuckled. "Nah, you probably just drowned him. Dragons are partial to wetness, don't you know?"

She let her hands slip over his firm chest. "And caves?"

"Mmm. Lucky dragon." His sparse chest hair was soft to the touch. She trailed a finger over the downward trail that ended below his belt, but he stalled her hand when it was on his belly. "Sorry. But we agreed that tonight was about you. Are you ready for part two?"

"Are you serious?"

"Hmm-hmm."

After two orgasms in one night, anything else was extra. She gave him her most wicked grin. "Bring it on."

50

He reached for the vase and extracted a small, dusky purple bloom. With the barely-opened tip he caressed the side of her breast with the cool, delicate petals, the fragile stamen, moving the flower until she felt the first tingles of excitement start again. The slow caress moved around her breast twice more before the center of the bud was twirled on her overly-sensitive nipple. The blur of purple swept against her dark skin, making tender kisses wherever it touched. His movements were slow and gentle, somewhere between a massage and the delicate touch of a feather.

"Oh... that... feels... gooooood...

He smiled, but his eyes were darkening with passion again. The blossom moved to the other breast for the same erotic treatment, while his free hand undid the tie of her robe from around her knees.

When the thin slip of material fell to the floor, he placed the flower on the counter, parted her thighs and stood between them to give her a lingering kiss on the lips.

This time it was different, it was more exploratory, slower. And just by the fact that she now had her thighs spread open, with him standing between them, she felt the kiss more intimately.

In no time at all, things were hot and heavy again and he pulled back.

His fingers moved between her legs to remove the sopping blue 'dragon,' and then he tugged her into a standing position.

51

When her legs proved to be wobbly, he lifted her and carried her to the couch, his strong arms seeming to be barely threatened by her weight.

"What are you up to?"

"Part two isn't over yet."

"What's part two?"

It didn't escape her notice that he placed her in the exact place she'd been in when she'd masturbated for him.

"I watched you," he said huskily, as he pushed the robe aside and parted her thighs again. The wetness on her labia glistened and the scent of feminine sex filled the air. "And I wanted to be your fingers, I wanted to hear those sounds you were making and I don't mean over the phone. I wanted to smell you. To taste you."

Sharonda felt the words work on her like a drug, making her feel sexy and wanton. She could see the large stain on his trousers where his ejaculation had left its mark. His renewed erection was growing there again and she suddenly felt selfish.

"James, if you want to get naked and—"

"No, no. In your diary you wanted the experience to be all about you, so let me do that, okay?"

She nodded.

"Geez, didn't put up much of an argument," he teased with a grin, his hands sliding up the fishnets to the garters.

"Well, I…"

His hands were moving up her legs from her shins. "Yes?"

"I..."

He lowered his head, his tongue licking her inner thigh. Once. Twice.

She fought for breath. "I, ah..."

The scrape of teeth sank into a soft nibble. Closer to her sex. Closer still, until his tongue extended a full lick on her exposed sex.

"Oh, Christ..."

"There you go again," he mumbled before aligning his mouth with her vulva and settling her legs on his shoulders. The kiss was carnal, and sinfully pleasurable as each stroke of his tongue and each suckle of his lips aroused different, newer sensations than the silken dragon ever had. If anything, the dragon had been a prelude to this moment, making the area more sensitive to his hungry mouth.

Sharonda felt carried by a tide, by James' strength, by the weakness of desire that threatened to make her come undone. With one hand clutching the cushion of the couch and the other holding his head, she arched her back and pointed her toes, feeling the heels scraping on the carpet. She closed her eyes and began to merge with the oral rhythm he was creating.

It seemed forever before he paused momentarily, then seconds later, she felt two cool round metallic balls slip past her nether lips and into her cervix.

"James?" she asked, peering breathlessly through her eyelids at him.

"Trust me," he said gruffly.

His mouth was back to French kissing her vagina, flicking the small vibrating balls inside her as if her body had become a pin ball machine. Each connecting hit brought on a greater shiver, and even though his hands held her buttocks, she found herself surging harder against his mouth, whimpering and moaning with building tension.

"Oh, God... Oh God! Oh!! Oh!!! James!!!" Ecstasy speared through her, from where his mouth was destroying her senses, licking up the lather of her pleasure, to where her nipples quivered, deep down to where the metallic balls knocked and hummed together.

He kept licking and licking until she felt like a spent, drowsy, mass of flesh. After a final tender kiss, he inserted two fingers and slipped the white and black balls out, making her gasp in the process. With a twist on each half, he turned them off.

As tired as she was, she saw his hand tremble and knew he was ready to discharge any minute. He wiped his face with the tail of his shirt, looking aroused and handsome as sin with his hand on the outline of his erection. She leaned forward and covered his hand with hers.

"You don't—"

"Come on. Give it to me. I want it."

There was no time to even unzip his trousers. He clamped

his hand over hers and stroked his long hard length three times before grunting from the force of his release. In her palm his penis twitched and the length of flesh strained in her grasp until the ejaculation darkened the stain further, making the wet ring wider.

When it was over, she leaned back and he laid his head on her belly, breathing heavily to recover. While she lay there, floating somewhere between sleep and reprieve, she heard him ask for the bathroom.

Already weary, she pointed in the general direction and lay on the couch for a more relaxed position.

In complete honesty, she meant to only rest her eyes for a minute. She heard the water running, then the slight squeak when he turned the faucet off, but after that, she wasn't even sure she heard the front door close when he left.

Chapter 6

"Helllloooo!" Aaliyah snapped her fingers in front of Sharonda's eyes. "Girl, you've been day dreaming ever since we got to the mall! What's up with that?"

Sharonda shrugged it off, catching their reflection as they walked past a jewelry store. "Nothing. I've just got stuff on my mind."

Aaliyah smacked her gum and gave her a look. "Like what? When we usually go shopping, we stack up on shoes and clothes and stuff. All you've been looking at are men's ties."

"I've got work on my mind. Besides, that tie I bought is a gift."

"Right, right."

"Work's been hectic. Some of us put in our eight and then some. Last week, I worked overtime every day but Friday." And the reasons she'd kept Friday to herself kept coming back to mind every time she spotted a tie!

"There you go again," Aaliyah said, waving her finger in a no-no fashion. "Did you get yourself a man and not tell me about it?"

Sharonda exhaled, blowing up her bangs. "I just told you I've been busy at work." Then seeing her friend open her mouth for another question, she interrupted, "Uh, check out those earrings."

Aaliyah took her cue and studied the gold hoop earrings with a critical eye. "Cute. I already have too many though."

"Yeah, me too. But maybe my sister would like them."

"Hmm. So, anyway, did you get yourself laid or something?"

"Aaliyah!"

Her friend cackled in her loud, good-natured way. "By the look on your face, it must be true. You're always so uptight. You could use a bit of man candy."

Sharonda chuckled but didn't deny it.

"So, how was it?"

"Good."

"That's all?"

"Damned good."

"Details, sister. Gimme details! How long is his—"

"Aaliyah!"

Her friend rolled her eyes, then waved her hand, indicating that Sharonda should spill the story.

"Okay, he's... just a friend."

"Right, right."

"And he... God, he..." Sharonda realized she'd stopped walking as she mentally searched for the right words.

"Must've been sweet if you can't describe it. Did he make you stutter or what?"

Sharonda felt her smile grow. "Y-Y-Yes."

Aaliyah raised her perfect eyebrows in a serious look and smacked the gum again. "What's his name?"

"Don't go there. You don't even know him."

"You're jealous too?"

Sharonda made a dismissing sound, then walked to the nearest clothes rack and assessed a sweater. Aaliyah moved next to her and held another sweater to her chest. "What do you think? Too pink? Bet it would be cute on you. You need to get away from those gray suits and low heels, girl."

"Hmm. What's wrong with my shoes?"

Aaliyah replaced the hanger on the rack. "You need some high-heels. Anyway, was it a one-night thing or what?"

Sharonda shrugged and fussed with the sweater before putting it back. "Two nights. I like him a lot. But... It's complex."

"The most important thing is that he's good in the sack, right?"

"I—Well, I guess."

"You guess?" Aaliyah tugged her arm and pulled her to a nearby bench. "What's with the 'I guess'?"

"Aaliyah, I love you like a sister, but you are getting to be nosy as hell."

Her friend merely blinked at her, silently reminding her

they were best friends.

Sharonda sighed. "We haven't had sex exactly. I mean, we were kinda talking and, you know, but all of a sudden, just when I thought we were going somewhere with it, he left a message on my answering machine today saying he'll be gone for a few days."

"Hold up." Aaliyah frowned and chewed her gum like a pro chomper. "I though you said sex was good."

"No, I said it was good... You know, solo."

Aaliyah's eyebrows hitched up even higher. "You're saying you took care of him?"

"No. He took care of me."

"Git out!"

"Serious."

"What is this brother's name?"

Sharonda smiled wryly. "None of your business, but if you've gotta know, it's James."

"James," Aaliyah said, as if trying out a foreign word. "Maybe he's got a cousin or something."

Sharonda shifted her heavy purse. "I thought you were dating Darnel?"

"That fool. Thought he could date me and two others."

"No! I'm sorry." Sharonda reached for her friend's hand.

"Don't be. I found out before my heart was in it. Had a pecker like a hazelnut too." Aaliyah indicated the size with her thumb and her pinkie.

Sharonda laughed, glad to see that her friend wasn't really hurt by the experience.

"So what's so special about this guy that puts stars in your eyes?" Aaliyah asked.

Sharonda felt the familiar warmth spread in her gut. "He's tall, dark and handsome. And he's an architect. Likes hiking, and has an obsession with gadgets."

"Hey, that can be fun—"

"And he found my diary—"

"What?"

"He read it—"

"Girl!"

"I know it. You know how it is, I wrote a few dreams and things like that. And now he says he wants to make them come true."

"Oh, goodness gracious!"

"Aaliyah, I was so scared, but at the same time, I wanted to see if he could, you know, live up to my expectations and... he did."

Aaliyah fanned herself with a discount flyer from her shopping bag. "Shooot, you're starting to fall for him, sister."

Sharonda automatically frowned. "James? No way—"

"Yes, way."

"You've got it wrong. I mean, I'm still wondering why he's doing it, you know? I mean, I know I'm not all that. But maybe he decided not to continue and that's why he left the message on my answering machine... Or maybe he's disappointed in me because I should've done something... I don't know!"

"I cannot believe you are complaining!" Aaliyah chuckled. But when she finally put down the paper she was fanning herself with, her eyes looked sad as she said, "Take it from me, Sharonda, if a man wants to fulfill my fantasies, or if he can just get the sex right, I'd keep him."

As all surprises go, Sharonda got hers when she entered the apartment complex and headed for the elevators. It had been two days since she'd last seen James. But he'd been there all along, in the dreams she replayed in the steam of her coffee, in the reflection of clouds. Every one of his facial expressions, every turn of his hands twirling his tie into that unforgettable shape became a sensuous memory.

Just yesterday, she'd called him twice and hung up every time the answering machine picked up.

And yet here he was, entering the elevator and pressing a button, holding what looked like an overnight bag in his hand.

Sharonda grinned and hurried toward him, but a blur of motion passed her with a squeal. "Jaaammeeessss!"

"Lucille?" The petite woman hurled herself into his arms, but she could see him grin as he hugged her tightly. When he laughed, his eyes suddenly made contact with Sharonda's, noticing her for the first time. The expression of being caught red-handed was cut off by the elevator doors as they closed on the couple.

"No!" Sharonda clenched her teeth, fighting a sharp sense of devastation mixed with an irrational, jealous dose of anger. He's gone for two days and then this? She forced her feet to move and ran to the elevator, punching the button, but it had already began its ascension.

"Damned bastard!" she bit off. Then, muttering more profanities, she turned to storm up the stairs to her apartment. Breathing in, breathing out, trying to stay calm. The smell of irises filled in the air, the beautiful display within sight from the front door. The reminder of what they'd shared pushed her anger notches higher.

Dropping her purse, keys and letters on the couch, she hurried to the balcony to remove the wind chime she'd set up that morning.

The old glass door was difficult to open. She wasted precious seconds trying to unfasten the safety locks, but when it did open, it slid back with a resonating slam. Sharonda balanced on a potted plant and wrestled the wind chimes from their stubborn hook, immediately silencing the fragile song. Across from her, she could see the light on in his apartment. Both he and the woman were watching!

Feeling wholly humiliated, Sharonda hurried inside when

he took a step out onto his balcony.

"Fool!" she mumbled to herself and she moved indoors, closing the glass door and whipping the curtain back into place. With anger, she dumped the chimes into the vine basket. Of course he was having a laugh at her expense. What had she been expecting?

"Going out of town on business, my ass!" she said heatedly, glaring accusingly at her answering machine. Her throat clogged and she swallowed hard, determined not to cry. So what if he was hugging that—that hussy! It was too familiar and intimate a hug to be just a recent acquaintance. Well, she'd had the best part of their brief relationship. It was nothing but two fake dates anyway.

"Oh, damn!" She winced, remembering the ivory-cream colored tie she'd mailed to him the day of his departure. At the time she'd thought it would make a perfect homecoming gift, a wonderful memento of the time they had shared. The golden moon-shaped tie clip had been added after endless deliberation. Aaliyah had warned her it was too soon for gifts and done the listen-to-me routine of rolling her eyes. Sharonda hadn't listened.

Damn!

The sudden shrill of the phone startled her and she stood beside it, angry and undecided. After the third ring, her answering machine picked up. James' voice filled the room like his presence. He sounded amazingly calm.

"Sharonda, pick up. I know you're there... pick up."

She muttered an obscenity and felt the sweet rush of anger streaming though her veins like venom. She had to be indifferent! She had to prove she could be blasé about their little fling, if that was even what it was. She wasn't about to settle for his pity!

She snatched the phone, trying to be as cool and collected as possible. "Look, James, I see you've found another... arrangement. Don't bother calling here again, okay? I understand. It was fun, but it's over. Keep the tie. Goodbye!"

She slammed the phone down and seconds later, it rang again. A flick of her thumb turned off the ringer and the answering machine.

Hadn't they talked about exclusivity about the same time they'd discussed architecture? He hadn't seemed like the type to double-dip in relationships. Or even triple-dip. Hell, there was no way she was going to do a threesome.

Fuck it! She hoped his dick withered from infection. It wasn't like she knew how good it worked anyway. The whole thing had been too good to be true.

Exhaling, she took off her gray, collarless jacket with the wide buttons in the front. The sensible black flat-heeled shoes, she kicked off, then pulled her white silk shirt from the plain gray skirt and began undoing the pearly buttons.

She paused halfway to raid the candy jar for gummy bears. Nothing commiserated better than the stuff. She had three of the chewy candies in her mouth when the doorbell rang. A quick peek through the peek-hole verified it was James.

"Sharonda. Come on, open the door."

Twice more he called and twice she ignored him, until finally she walked away, only to hear keys jingle and see the door swing open. He was dressed as professionally as the last time he'd stepped through her doorway, except this time his clothes were a dark olive green and a bit travel-weary. Or maybe it wasn't travel that had wrinkled them, but that short loud hussy.

"That's illegal!" she snarled. "There are tenant laws! You can't just let yourself into people's apartments without their permission!"

He clasped the keys in his palm, looking resigned. "I had to, you wouldn't open the door."

"I'm filing an official complaint with the—"

"She's my sister."

"What?" Her fingers froze from where they had been actively trying to re-button the shirt, attempting to hide the view of her cleavage.

"That woman who squealed like a banshee when I was in the elevator," he said, patiently spelling it out. "She's my little sister. I haven't seen her in seven months and well, she was glad to see me. I was glad to see her too."

Sharonda paused, then huffed. "Right, you expect me to believe that?"

"Glad you asked. She's sitting by my phone if you want to talk to her."

Sharonda gave up on the button and settled her hands on her hips. Taking advantage of her speechlessness, he walked over to her phone and dialed, handing her the receiver.

"I don't want it—"

"Take it." He sounded as annoyed as she felt, so she took it, even avoiding his fingers.

"Hello? Hi, I'm Lucille. James said you might call," was the first thing Sharonda heard, followed by a friendly dissertation of James as a sibling, his parents, older sister and ending with how she, Lucille, was an unplanned baby.

As the voice yammered in her ear, Sharonda saw James' eyes lower to her cleavage, assess, then travel all the way to her toes.

"Do you want to know anything else?" Lucille finally asked.

"No, thanks." After polite good-byes Sharonda hung up the phone.

"That wasn't necessary." she said, still feeling awkward.

"Really? The look on your face seemed to require an explanation."

Sharonda sighed, feeling embarrassed and yet justified.

James' voice was just the tiniest bit huskier as he said, "Thanks for the tie."

Unsettled, she crossed her arms across her chest and their

eyes locked. Should she tell him how yesterday, she'd taken his other tie for a ride on the spin cycle. Every jostle turned the two metallic balls into power thrusts, and with the slick texture of the silk dragon she'd come like a rocket.

Would he accept that for an apology?

The silence stretched and the unmistakable look of passion settled in his eyes. "Come here."

"You probably think I overreacted."

"Just... come here."

After a deep breath she went to him, each step making a soft sound on the carpet. She stopped just an arm's distance from him.

"Closer."

She moved nearer until her breasts almost touched his shirt. She licked her lips, eyeing the sexy curve of his lips.

"Are you going to put the wind chime back out?" he asked, his voice sounding smoky.

"Mmm. Maybe."

His smile widened. "Would this convince you?" The kiss he placed on her lips was a light flick of his tongue on her bottom lip, a fleeting pulse of his lips upon hers, a soft negligent nibble on the corner of her mouth. A mutual second where they both inhaled the same breath.

"James..." The word came out hungrily and he answered it by slanting his mouth over hers and kissing her as if he'd been deprived of the intimacy for too long. Her arms went around his neck, his arms twined around her and the kiss blazed into a long-tongued event.

After what felt like an eternity, he pulled back, breathing heavily. Sharonda opened her eyes and tried to gather her wits, but still the world seemed to be spinning, with James at her center.

"I can't stay," he said quietly, regretfully. "My sister's in town for a few days. I promised I'd spend some time with her."

Sharonda nodded.

He touched her cheek. "I'll call you."

She let her hands slide down his torso.

His eyes spoke of what the call would mean; the intimacy would involve the diary; the physicality would no longer be one-sided. A world of yearning unraveled further in her gut when he placed a kiss in the center of her right palm then moved toward the door. "And Sharonda?"

"Hmm?"

"I wouldn't cheat on you. I know some of your boyfriends did. But I won't."

She didn't know what to say. She wanted to trust him. Really wanted to.

"Later." He said the words as if he also wished that the hours would disappear and allow them the instance they craved.

"Later," she agreed.

Chapter 7

For the next two days, James devoted his spare time to his sister, who was just back from one of her many trips to Tanzania. Her African import business was thriving, and she was relaying one of her adventures at the Kenyan Tusk and Panga bar when his mind began to drift... to Sharonda.

The waiting was getting unbearable. The yearning was stretching under his skin like an aphrodisiac every time he thought of her. He wanted her with such a base carnal yearning that he wondered if he'd be able to properly restrain himself when the time came to consummate. Even now, the recurring words he'd seen in her diary taunted him, becoming his needs.

I need... I want... I crave... I wish...

"You're not listening to a word I'm saying," Lucille complained.

"Of course I was," he lied.

She stopped in the middle of chopping the celery and gave him a disbelieving look. "Then what was I saying?"

He turned back to the sink to rinse the lettuce leaves. "Something about lions, malachite and Zimbabwe."

A small section of celery hit him squarely in the back of the head. "Not even close."

He laughed and returned to stand beside her, the lettuce in a bowl. "Okay, okay. Sorry, sis. What were you saying?"

The knife made a staccato sound as she expertly diced a length of cucumber. "She's heavy on your mind, isn't she?"

"Who?"

Lucille rolled her eyes. "Don't pretend. You can't go for five minutes without getting that blank look on your face."

"Intellects are born with this look."

"So are morons," she quipped with a grin. "What gives?"

He sighed, trying to find just the right words to explain and yet not reveal much.

"You haven't called her since I've been here. I think that's odd," Lucille said, watching him closely.

"We have an agreement."

"Like what?"

"Like none of your business."

"Hey, I just want to make sure you don't walk right into heartbreak city."

He smirked, since he knew it annoyed her. "I'm the older sibling here."

"And that counts for didley."

"You're talking like she's a barracuda or something."

Lucille waved the deadly knife in a casual dismissing fashion. "They come in all shapes and sizes."

He was about to respond, then thought better of it and kept his mouth shut.

"Don't frown like that," Lucille chastised. "I just think it's strange that in the two days I've been here, all three of us haven't spent time together, yet on that first day, you practically ran over there to explain who I was. So, is she someone important to you or is she just a temporary thrill."

James found he didn't have an honest answer to that, and so with more force than he'd intended, he replied, "Sis, like I said, that's none of your business."

Lucille raised her eyebrows and changed the subject, which was a subtle sign of forgiveness, but the question had been planted deep in his mind, demanding an answer.

Ever since the elevator incident, Sharonda had started taking the stairs again. But today the steps seemed endless. Halfway up the first floor, she thought she heard the sound of chimes at a distance, but it wasn't until she was in her apartment, peering through the balcony that she spotted wind chimes hanging from James' balcony, the design identical to hers.

Her heart beat double time, and she found herself grinning hugely. But that was nothing compared to her reaction when she heard the simple message on her answering machine.

"There's no moon out tonight, but page seventy-seven looks tempting. What do you say?"

She raced to the bedroom, grabbed her diary and flipped to the specific page.

"I can see the moon outside my window, and the night is like a mouth, wide open, about to swallow it whole. I wish I could be devoured and ravished like that. Yes, that corny old-fashioned word, ravished, when I really mean fucked! Except I also mean ravished. Fuck-ravished. Done. Well-done and thank you very much.

I want to feel that lightning until I feel my toes curl with an orgasm, until I won't have to fake anything, until I have to beg whomever it is to stop."

"Oh my goodness!" The time had come.

She glanced at the clock. It was six thirty. If she bathed, blow dried her hair and microwaved a TV dinner; she could be ready in about an hour and a half.

As it turned out, she was too restless to sit in the tub for any length of time, so instead she scrubbed herself thoroughly, knowing every inch of skin was going to be fair game. Once dry, she brushed her teeth, applied faint make-up, and went about blow-drying her hair, which took longer than expected but helped calm her nerves.

She rifled through her lingerie drawer and pulled out her most recent purchase a black lace number with delicate see-through panties and red accent garters to match. And, of course, the black high-heeled shoes.

The silky smoky-black nylons matched the sheer robe and by the time she looked in the mirror, she wondered why she'd never dressed this way for any of her boyfriends before. Sure, she was no size ten, but she felt like a diva! Maybe because she'd never felt so sexy before.

She flattened her trembling hand over her stomach, too nervous to even think of microwaving the TV dinner. Instead, she picked on the mixed fruit salad, popping diced watermelon and grapes into her mouth.

Would calling him now be too soon? Maybe she should wait until eight o'clock? The chimes outside taunted and she looked over at his apartment and spotted him.

James looked like he'd stepped out of the shower. A small towel was snug around his hips while he used another to dab his shaved head. As if sensing her gaze, he turned toward her. Without the binoculars, she couldn't be certain, she thought he gave her one of those slow, smoldering smiles before waving.

She waved back, admiring his natural pose that was so elementary masculine. It made her want him in ways that sank claws of need into her gut. She wondered what he smelled like. What soap and cologne did he use? More than that she wanted to hear the sexy rumble of his voice, to see him up close. To feel him. Up close. To experience all the subtle nuances of a dream lover coming to life. Up. Close.

"Buck up," she grumbled to herself, knowing she was setting high expectations. "He's only human. He's only human. Sex is just sex."

He placed his hand by his ear, signaling "call me."

She reached for the phone and dialed. He picked up right away, but by then, she noticed, he had his binoculars in hand.

"Very sexy," he said after a low whistle. "I take it page seventy-seven is a go?"

"Definitely."

"What time?"

"Now?"

He inhaled slowly, letting her answer hang in the air for a few seconds. "Close the curtain, honey. I'll be right there."

This time when the doorbell rang, she answered it.

But just like before, when he stepped over her threshold, she watched him in awe. There were no words exchanged, no bane pleasantries. Her eyes locked with his, seeing the depth of passion there and melting into it.

Then with the door closed against her back, he leaned toward her, his white t-shirt and soft jeans just inches from her body. There was something about his gaze, the admiration and promise there, a strangely balanced mixture of impatience and calmness.

Sharonda broke the silence by murmuring his name and that was all it took. His mouth swooped down on hers for a slow tender kiss that cooked in degrees, lengthening in discovery, leisurely with absolute expertise.

His tongue licked into her mouth to stroke and take, curled and sucked on her lips and tasted every recess, and drank as if she were unquenchable.

She couldn't even remember kisses lasting this deliciously long in high school. And still his body remained separated by inches, his mouth the only thing touching her. On and on their mouths merged, as if in a dance, discovering, taking hungrily, then surrendering.

When his lips finally moved to her neck, a shiver passed over her, slipping into her moan, low and deep. Already her breath was coming in gasps and her mind felt passion-muddled.

When she peered through her lashes at him, he pulled back a bit, but his breathing was as irregular as her own. Over his shoulder, she noticed the clock on the wall. Christ, he'd been kissing her for twenty-six minutes?

"You look gorgeous," he said, taking a moment to look over her entire ensemble. "It's very sexy... but I guess I've said that already."

She couldn't help smiling at the utter sincerity in his voice. "You look very sexy too... Even that banana in your pocket."

His lips turned upward, becoming a lusty grin. "What can I say, I'm happy to see you."

Knowing she had his full attention, she passed her hand over the blatant erection that threatened to undo his button fly. James groaned, a mixture of restraint and arousal.

His hand cupped hers and his hips moved to thrust against her palm in long strokes. Then with a stronger grip, he pulled her hand away, moving it next to her face while he nibbled on her earlobe. "I think we should at least move from the door, don't you?"

She felt bold, salacious, and very much a new woman. It gave her the initiative to ask, "How about the bedroom?"

The smoldering fire in his eyes flared. "Your wish is my command."

"Any wish?"

"Any wish at all."

Taking his hand, she led the way to her bedroom, where she already had several votive candles illuminating the room. The sturdy four-poster bed had been covered with a thin scarf-like overhang that added to the soft dim lights, gave the room a lush feel.

James looked around, and she noticed the mischievous approval in his eyes when he spotted her vanity mirror reflecting their position by the bed. She'd never thought to use it for sex, but she suddenly realized that James would.

He reached for the tie of her sheer robe.

She stalled him with a touch on his chest. "I think your t-shirt needs to come off first."

"Then take it off me."

Her hands slid to where the shirt was tucked into his jeans. With her hands holding fistfuls of the material, she tugged upward, slowly, enjoying the view of tight black skin that was revealed.

Moving her wrists over the warm skin, she touched the outline of muscle and form, then pushed the material upwards again. When the shirt brushed past his heart, his breathing became deeper and she released the shirt to run her palms over his male nipples while licking the pulse of his heartbeat below her lips.

"Hands up," she mumbled and he complied.

She took her time, running her hands on his back and brushing her lace-cupped nipples against his chest. Little by little, the shirt went over his shoulders, his elbows, his wrists, then fell unnoticed onto the bed. The smell of his warm skin and his faint deodorant filled her lungs and when his arms went around her, she spent another breathless moment lost in a kiss.

Finally his lips moved to her neck, teasing the robe from her collarbones and off her shoulders. Every movement of his lips was feeding the familiar storm that moved upon her skin like shivers. His hands caressed hungrily, restlessly, from the round globes of her buttocks to her waistline, to cup and torment her sensitive breasts. Each time, they explored further, going down to her thighs to squeeze there and gather her to him in a mock thrust, then traveling back up her torso almost to her armpits. And still his mouth never left hers. Each touch, each thrust was brought about as if he had all the time in the world.

When his fingers gently squeezed her nipples, she groaned a weak and honeyed moan that snaked through her body like the robe slipping to the carpet. She clung to him and closed her eyes, whispering, "You're making me dizzy."

"Hmmm." His mouth found her left breast and sucked the soft underside despite the lacy barrier.

"Oh!" Her knees grew weaker and the fire in her womb was blazing steadily hotter.

He suckled and withdrew, nipped and withdrew, tongued and breathed on the sensitive flesh, making her bite her lip to keep from crying out. Tipped back the way she was, his hips rocked against hers, until she was sure her wetness was creaming the front of his jeans.

"James, please!" She swayed and he held her tight, letting the body contact absorb the heat of need. "I can't even stand straight."

He released her slowly, then reached for his discarded shirt, looping it over the overhead beam of the bed.

"Grab hold of this," he ordered, raising her hands to his shirt.

Sharonda gripped the material, catching a glimpse in her vanity mirror of her vulnerable position. His head was immediately buried in her cleavage and his wide palms were cupping her buttocks. His muscular arms rippled, his shoulders and back strong and curved as he rocked against her.

Then the vision disappeared when his fingers slipped through the soaked lace of her crotch and plunged into the slick heat of her vagina.

"James—!" Eyes tightly shut, she gripped the shirt, tugging upward to thrust against his hand, gritting her teeth at the most decadent pleasure of initial penetration.

"Do you like that?" he whispered hoarsely.

"Yessss."

Again and again, his clever fingers plunged into her vagina and rubbed against her clitoris. His teeth tugged the lace from her breasts and his mouth latched onto the exposed flesh with wanton yearning. The combination was incredibly effective and even as she squeezed the shirt in her hands, she felt the surge of the oncoming orgasm gathering momentum.

"James, now!"

A lopsided smile graced his lips. "Not yet."

"Now, please!"

Her sensitive nipple suffered another oral caress. "It's way too soon, honey. I—"

"Damnit!" The hitch in her voice betrayed her and she felt as if she was either going to cry from desperation or die from

Delilah Dawson

frustration.

"All right, sugar," he murmured hoarsely. His hands loosened from around her to remove his clothing. When she opened her eyes, she saw him undoing the buttons of his jeans and shuck them down to mid thigh, slipping on a condom. As she had suspected, he wore no underwear and his firm, muscular buttocks and thighs were a sensuous sight.

His magnificent erection sprang forth, the thick black trunk of it straining hard in the direction of her crotch. She looked between their bodies to see the tight plum head of his cock nudging the lace opening of her panties and nuzzle closer.

"Like this?" he asked huskily, using his thumb to stroke her clit while his gloved penis teased at her portal. She couldn't even stammer a response, so he decided to suckle on her breasts again.

"J—J—" God! He was driving her crazy.

His cock pushed its tight way inside and her panting mixed with his brief moan. She barely opened her eyes.

"Cooper, please..." she begged, seeing the matching desire in his eyes.

"Hold tight," he whispered and she strengthened her grip on the shirt.

With their eyes holding fast, he lifted her slightly, so that her nylon-clad legs wrapped around him, the high-heels crossing over his spine as he lowered her firmly onto his hardened shaft. The shivers that had been coursing through her body ripped through her as if his penis was the magnetic source to her body's alluring pull. A keen pleasure pain matched the sheathing thoroughness of his possession, making her arch her back.

"Take it," he said gruffly, his words sounding both like a command and at the same time, like encouragement.

"Oh... oh..." she whimpered as she slid the last tight inch on him, completely impaled. The slit lace of her panties pulled tightly on her clitoris. Firmly holding her with one arm, his other slipped between their bodies to rub her clitoris while lowering his head to sink a love bit on her breast.

Sharonda couldn't hold back the startled womb-twitching waves of pleasure and she came unexpectedly, in a hard orgasm that made strangling sounds in her throat.

Yet he didn't stop, and for that moment, she felt as if the pulsating in her gut would stretch out indefinitely, trembling in her chest like the crest of a sneeze, gripping her vaginal muscles that clasped him in responding spasms.

And just like that, between one slow blink and another, she rode out the fascinating pleasure, her fingers numbing as she gripped his shirt tighter.

Unbelievable!

It had never happened like that before, never at such a rush of breath and certainly not after just one thrust.

There was no recovery time, only the surreal moment of

the mind-blowing orgasm and the return of sensation when he began to pump in wilder, blunter thrusts.

She could barely hold on to his shirt. She felt like he would rip her in two and yet as if he was taking her to the summit of sensation all over again.

In the aftermath of her pleasure, she could feel his control start to slip. His hips moved more insistently, becoming rigid plowing. Glimpses in the mirror revealed his sweat-slicked back, the rolling clench of his buttocks under the crossed high heels, the pulling grip of his hands on her hips where her nylons were slipping to mid-thigh. The helpless expression on her face, and the way her hands looked like they were tied by his shirt.

The slick sounds of sex and the smell of lust blended with each erogenous sensation. Even the force of his thrusts seemed to pull the surrounding vaginal lace into her, causing new, erotic friction. Then the rhythm crested and her trembling arms could barely hold on to the shirt overhead. She clung to him as his ejaculation fired hot and plentiful deep inside.

"Sha...rhonda!" he ground between his teeth, grunting his hard release. His shirt slipped from her fingers and they toppled onto the bed, nailing one final unexpected thrust that almost sent them crashing over the edge of the mattress.

Breathing was a hard and heavy exercise, but they gasped in air through parted lips, puffing as if they'd survived a marathon. His head was next to hers, his body curved over her while her legs remained wrapped around him. She opened her eyes to find him looking at her in the mirror, noticing the sexy contrast of her nylons and high heels on his bare back even as his jeans sagged around his knees.

"Well," he said when he could finally talk. "I did that all wrong."

She pushed bangs from her eyes and turned to him, receiving a moist kiss in the process. "I don't think you did a single thing wrong."

"I'd planned to have more control," he admitted. His hand moved to touch her cheek, his eyes filled with a mixture of wariness and tenderness. "Are you okay?"

She smiled and sighed indulgently. "I always wonder exactly what that question means."

He seemed fascinated with the movement of her lips. "I didn't want to be too rough."

He couldn't have been more perfect! "You weren't."

His finger touched the corner of her lip. "Hmm."

"Except that my arms are weak from holding on to your shirt."

James' grin widened. "You said you didn't want vanilla sex, so you can't complain about that."

She chuckled. "I see. I'm afraid to ask what else you have in mind."

Deep inside her, he flexed phallic muscles, causing movement of his semi-soft penis.

"Anything… Everything…"

"Like?"

"Let me show you what else I had in mind," he said and together they rolled to the center of the bed. He magically had a condom in his hand…

She hadn't known sex could be like that. Like a sport. Like a decadent meal. Like the best kind of erotic discovery.

It kept amazing her to what lengths his mouth would go to lick her for her pleasure, discovering what evoked her deepest sexual response. His hands followed suit. Then his body, skin on skin…

Foreplay became a kind of sensual torture where she could show him everywhere she wanted to be touched, her hand over his, leading him boldly.

"Here?" he asked in her ear, while their joined hands moved down her ribs.

Her reply was a breath. "Yes."

Her thighs. Between them. Then lower, bending her knee so they could reach her ankles. Her arches. Touching and questioning along the way.

"Right here?"

"Yes, just like"

"Like this?"

"Ahh… yesss…"

"You have to show me…"

And when his hard erection finally pushed into her again, she lay on her side, reveling at the different depth of penetration, the sensitivity. He'd knelt with one of her legs stretched upwards so that her ankle rested on his shoulder and the other leg slipped between his, feeling the weight of his testicles on her inner thigh. He'd taken his time sliding in and out of her that way, licking her amazingly sensitive ankles through the nylons and brushing his knuckles over her pubic hair...

Then later, half asleep, he made a long, arduous trek starting from her inner thighs, where he began by removing the garters, using his teeth to pull the nylons all the way to her toes.

Then on the way up, he sucked on her toes, nibbled on her arches, French kissed her ankles, her calves, even her knees.

"Turn over," was his brief command. Sharonda flipped onto her belly, allowing him to continue with the back of her knees, licking, nipping and kissing until she was grinding her hips into the mattress. He took his ever-loving sweet time removing every scrap of lace she wore, until there were no more barriers. Nothing but skin on skin.

He grunted appreciatively about the roundness of her buttocks in his hands, massaging them and leaning his chest closer so his mouth could reach her spine. And oh that mouth! Licking and nipping slowly all the way upward.

She squirmed. He followed. They kissed in that awkward half-turned embrace. Then a sharp nip led to light wrestling on the bed, but in the end, she found herself pinned with her breasts to the wallpaper, knees on the pillows, back arched, and she didn't care that he had somehow won.

❧

They slept solidly for an hour. Then when they awoke, James made love to her all over again, their skin covered with a thick sheen of sweat. Every thrust was plundered into her semi-raw passage.

"Oh, James! Oh!"

"Beautiful... I haven't masturbated for days," he confessed huskily, as if he had to admit why he was so horny. His hands slipped between the wall and her body, to fondle her breasts and then to gently squeeze her clit. "For days... I was saving up for this. Just thinking of you. Wanting this..."

The clock blurred out of focus and time spun.

He took her with her thighs open wide, then later with her legs crossed. He took her with his inquisitive mouth, redis-covering her every erogenous zones. Then later, when he sat weak-kneed on the family heirloom chair, she straddled him and rode him like a cowgirl with her heart set on the prize.

It wasn't until absolute exhaustion settled in that they slept for a while more.

Chapter 8

It was three-seventeen in the morning when she opened her eyes and peered at the bedside clock. Sharonda felt his arms slip lower on her waistline, and the hard nudge of his erection pushed insistently into her vagina.

When she flinched involuntarily, James eased out, his voice was an apologetic mumble. "Sorry, sugar."

Still half-asleep, she turned around and cuddled into him. "It's just— I'm a bit sore."

"Hmmm."

Her eyes grew heavy and she must've dozed again because when she woke up, it was to hear his grunt as he lifted her in his arms. Vaguely, she became aware that he was carrying her to the bathroom. He nuzzled her ear, calling her lazy bones under his breath and placed her into a bathtub filled with warm water.

Whatever remnants of sleep she had left, faded completely at the contact of water and she jerked, which caused her to fall in with a splash.

"You!" she gushed.

"Yes?" He slipped in with her before she could work up an

Delilah Dawson
answer. His weight displaced the water and raised the level to mere inches from the lip of the old claw-foot tub.

Words seemed inappropriate when she suddenly realized what he was doing. She'd written about this! Of just lounging in a tub served up by her dream lover. How could she describe how she felt after he'd fulfilled another fantasy?

Touched that he would go to such lengths, she could only say, "Thanks."

His eyes gleamed as he said, "You're welcome."

Sharonda filled her hands with the fragrant bath water. "You know you're going to end up smelling like freesia too."

He flashed his wicked grin. "I guess I'll have to do my best to sweat it off."

She laughed and lightly splashed him. Then looking around, she noticed he'd placed several candles around the sink, creating a soft golden light that reflected in the mirror. The warm water actually felt incredibly good, the steam joining the delicate freesia smell that filled the air.

Sharonda slipped into the space between his thighs and leaned back against his chest, exhaling a moment of pure bliss. Her head rested by his neck and when he chuckled, she felt the rumble against her back. Almost absently, he ran his hands idly over her body, in a sensual caress more than with any sexual intent.

"My hair is a total mess," she said out of the blue, the water making a soft sound as she raised her hand to try to control

88

the crazy hair.

"Understandably."

"Meaning?"

"I had to hold on to something when I had you squirming and begging me to— Ugh!" James rubbed the rib she elbowed. Peripherally, she saw his smile even though he muttered, "Crazy woman."

Next to the small towel rack was a stool with two drinks. He handed her one saying, "Here's a little remedy I whipped up. Coconut and pineapple are well known to heal muscle aches."

She took a deep sip from the straw. "Delicious."

He gulped down half the contents, stealing an ice cube from his glass and lazily toying with it over her skin, taking it around her nipples and then underwater to her belly button where it melted completely.

"Relax," he said when her back began to arch. "You're just going to lie here and relax while I soap you up."

True to his word, he used the liquid soap and soft wash-cloth to touch her everywhere his hands could easily reach. After a while, he abandoned the wash cloth.

"Open your thighs," he said.

She raised her legs so that they rested on the edge of the tub, leaving her thighs parted, her sex completely exposed. His nimble fingers lingered at the apex, swirling the water in a cleaning motion, then slipped into her love-bruised vagina.

"Relax," he murmured, caressing her as slowly as if he were fondling her breasts. Outside the wind chimes were a distant and delicate song.

"It's too sensitive," she confessed after a moment.

"Okay." His fingers slipped out of her raw passage but his hardening erection pushed against her spine.

"James, I could, um, wash you if you like."

"I like."

Taking her time, she too used the washcloth over his body, enjoying the simple pleasure of touching his skin in the water. When she touched his manhood, his eyes drooped and even though he hadn't moved a muscle, his body tensed.

"James, I could think of another way to—"

"Shh, I'm not like that. I don't really need sex right now. You just make me hard." He tipped her face toward his and kissed her, long and languidly. There was something about the tenderness of the kiss that impressed her. He made no demands, just kissed her the way someone would drink from life-giving water, and yet as if whiling away the minutes on a most enjoyable pastime.

When it ended, she realized, she'd half turned. Studying the velvety brown hues of his pupils, she ran her hand under the water, over his chest. "James... I don't know how to thank you. I mean about everything."

He didn't smile as she had expected, but his eyes were warm with intensity and eloquent in the following silence.

When he finally spoke, he said, "Believe me, the feeling is mutual."

Her fingers remained in the soft curly hair of his chest."Well, I'd still like to return the favor someday,"

This time he did smile, a wicked devilish turn of the lips that came with a wink. "Yeah?"

"Don't you have fantasies too?" she asked and tweaked his chest hairs playfully.

"Of course."

"Why don't you tell me about them?"

He gently doused some water on the slope of her arm in an absent gesture. "I— The— Oh, man," he sighed. "I can't quite decide on my favorite."

"How about writing them in a journal for me?"

He gave it some thought, then shook his head. "I don't think so. My fantasies should have different rules."

"Like what?"

"Like maybe I'll give you hints."

"Hints? Okay."

"I like spontaneity, so it's kinda hard to plan that, right?" he teased.

"Mmmm." Sharonda couldn't hold back a yawn.

"Am I boring you, sugar?"

"No! Not at all. Tell me more."

"Hmm, let me think for a minute..."

But for the second time, she fell asleep on him, waking

when the water started to get uncomfortably cold.

"Oh, James. I'm sorry. I didn't realize I was so tired."

"Don't worry about it," he replied groggily.

They toweled off and crawled into her bed, cuddling up and sleeping like children.

When Sharonda awoke, it was to the scent of cologne and coffee. She peered through her eyelids at James to find him fully dressed in a three-piece black conservative suit. She felt his hot whisper in her ear when he said, "I have to go."

Not entirely awake yet, she mumbled something and he chuckled. "It's almost nine o'clock, woman."

"Nine? In the morning?" She popped upright, gripping the sheets to her chest. "Lord, that's late! I'll make you coffee—" Her words failed when she noticed more clearly that he was ready for business. He'd obviously gone back to his apartment to change and maybe even for his own coffee.

"Go ahead. I'll wait in the kitchen," he promised, his eyes warming. "I have a few minutes still."

Sharonda jumped and raced to her bathroom, taking a shower and toweling off in record time. Was this how it was going to be?

By the time she walked into the kitchen, she felt somewhat composed in her gray suit and yellow shirt, but underneath, her body was still tender from the night of lovemaking. And even after everything they had done, she felt suddenly unsure of herself.

"I got a call this morning," he said, his hands in his pockets, pulling the jacket to the side. He looked like a model posing in a classic definition of style. And to think that just hours ago his body had been on her, his long fingers searching and caressing, his tongue and lips tracing her body in ways no other man ever had, feeling—

"Sharonda?"

"Ah, sorry," she turned away to reach for the pot of coffee, her cheeks betraying her with a heated blush. "You said you got a call?"

"I'm flying out on business tonight. I'll be back in two days."

"Oh." The sugar dropped carelessly into her mug.

Where was this leading? "Okay." What else could she say?

She felt his arms come around her and felt the touch of his lips by her ear. It was not an explanation, but it felt like a reassurance.

"Purely business," he said, as if sensing her questions.

"You don't owe me explanations," she said, lying through her teeth while concentrating on stirring.

James paused in the act of nuzzling her ear lobe. "I do if I expect the same of you." The tone in his voice made her look up at him.

His wristwatch beeped and he stepped back. "I'm going to be late if I don't leave now."

"Alright."

The kiss was familiar as it played on her lips, but she realized he too sensed the restraint of morning-after reality.

"Do you need a ride to the airport?" she asked when she could finally speak.

"No... but maybe you can pick me up when I get back?"

"Sure, just let me know when."

A ghost of a smile touched his lips and when he bent his head to kiss her a second time. The yearning was surging back through her veins.

"Last night was beautiful," he said, his voice intimate and filled with recollection.

"Yes..." Did he have to go?

"I'll call," he promised.   Seconds later, he was gone.

Chapter 9

It was late in the day by the time the meeting was over. James looked around the board room, glad that he would be part of the latest Milan Complex project. Nonetheless, he'd been surprised by how often his mind had wandered during the discussion, leading him to thoughts of Sharonda, her dark tea skin gleaming in candlelight, eyes half-closed, begging him, tearing the vowels in his name with her moans.

"So, it's agreed then!" Mr. Blake said in a loud voice.

Though James barely restrained a startled jerk, he had the sense to add his agreement to the chorus of his partners.

When everyone left, James lingered in the board room for a moment of privacy, then found himself impatiently reaching for the phone, dialing her number from memory.

"Hello?" Her voice was the polite curiosity of the woman who liked to wear gray suits, the one who was reserved and lonely, his teenage blind date.

"Hey, sugar," he said, deliberately making his voice lewd and husky. "Whatcha wearin'?"

Her welcoming chuckle was that of the seductress beneath the cool façade. Her voice became hush and sultry. "Go-go boots and a leather thong."

James laughed at her bold reply. "Hmmm, really?"

"No!... And you?"

"None of the above," he retorted, still chuckling.

The laughter settled into a comfortable silence, then she asked, "How's business?"

"Routine." He could hear the wind chimes in the background and smiled as he stared at a landscape print on the wall. Miss me? Should he ask? Instead he asked, "How about you?"

"The same."

He could hear the curiosity in her voice too. The uncertainty of how much to ask. So like careful dancers, they discussed the weather, the news, small talk about his business...until words became hands, touching and breaching the distance.

"What time should I pick you up?" she asked.

He loved the huskier pitch of her voice. "I arrive at seven-fifteen on Southwest Airlines."

"Okay. Um, any... special requests?"

He remained staring at the watercolor landscape print, one hand at his hip while an erection throbbed in his pants. "Yes. I'd like to play truth or dare with you."

Her tense exhale was like static on the phone. "Okay."

"What will it be?"

Sharonda was quiet for a moment, then said, "Dare."

He took a sip of cold water from his glass nearby. "I dare you to live out another of your fantasies, one you haven't written down. One I don't know."

He heard the soft sounds of what he would bet was her robe, wishing he could feel it against his face.

"This time was supposed to be your fantasy," she said, with only a slight hesitation.

"I'm into spontaneity. Are you game?"

He heard the sound of chimes so clearly, he knew she was toying with them. "Okay. You're on."

Outside the office James could hear the receptionist closing up. He cleared his throat. "I'll see you tomorrow then?"

"Most definitely."

The breathlessness of her voice leaked passion through his veins. He reveled in it for a moment. "I can hardly wait. See you then. Goodnight."

"Goodnight."

The airport was crowded with busy passengers and James found himself seeing entirely too many people blocking his search for Sharonda. But when he finally spotted her, he almost stopped walking.

The dowdy, gray-suit woman was gone. In her place was a sleek business woman. Her hair was fashioned in an elegant coiffure, pearls gleamed from her ears and decorated her throat. She wore a seal-brown trench coat, cinched tightly at the waist but falling down to her ankles. It revealed a cream-colored shirt with a soft collar at her neck.

James was speechless. Her profile was absolutely the most knockout, no nonsense, sexy look he'd ever seen.

Where her arms were crossed, the French cuffs revealed her hands and fire engine red nails. The color matched her lipstick. He was glad he'd decided to wear his jacket to hide his immediate response to her.

He stepped up to where she leaned against a pillar, an invitation on her lips and a search for approval in her eyes. Her high heels almost brought them to eye level.

"Hi," she said, her voice low and husky.

"Hi yourself."

Man, when she looked at him like that, it just made him crazy! Suddenly, there, in front of everyone, she reached for his tie to tug him closer and kissed him with that sweet red mouth, stealing a kiss with the most careful restraint.

Placing one hand on her hip, he inhaled her exotic perfume of woman and warmth, finding it hard to kiss her back with the same restraint she was showing. Damn, but he'd missed her!

Amazing. He'd never wanted a woman this fast, this badly. Every instinct in him wanted to hurl his briefcase behind him, close out the world and make love to her right there against the pillar.

"We should go," she finally said against his lips.

He didn't reply, but instead stepped back and let her lead the way to her car. Hand in hand, they made it through the busy hallways. All the while he was aware of the click-click of her high heels, of the warmth of her grasp in his, of the long trench coat brushing his clothes.

Once in the parking garage, he couldn't wait any more. He pushed her against the door of her slick black Mercedes and kissed her hungrily, trying not to let the rush of passion rule him. But he couldn't gobble up enough of her mouth, their tongues tangling as if they were sharing the same candy. Easy, he warned himself. Take it easy.

Holding firm to this resolve he nonetheless found himself untying the trench coat to slip his hands inside.

"Christ," he whispered, when his hands encountered her naked butt, where the tail of her shirt barely reached. Moving upward, he reached under the soft material to caress her equally naked breasts. Moving a palm downward revealed the nylons ended mid thigh. He lowered his hands to caress her firm buttocks and thighs, but no more. Definitely no more. At least for the moment.

Her quivering sigh filled his ears. He nipped at her earlobe. "Naughty, naughty, Sharonda. Just shirt and these thigh-highs. Very nice."

She inhaled unsteadily. "Don't forget the pearls and

heels," she added, her hands busy moving to his hips, then down his abdomen to touch his erection.

"Pearls. And heels. Yes."

And when they kissed again, he didn't care about heels or anything else but the need to bury himself between her willing thighs. To make her his. To brand her with their lovemaking until she would never think of another man but him again.

A tiny unsuppressed part of his brain complained wildly that he was falling in deeper into the relationship. That was not the agreement!

James immediately stifled the thought, forgetting everything but her alluring voice, breathing his name.

Somewhere in the parking garage, a car honked and the echo resonated loudly. Seconds later, he realized things were going to get out of hand unless they found some privacy.

Wordlessly, he did a quick pat of her pockets and extracted the car keys. It took only seconds to re-tie the trench coat, his lips brushing hers with nothing more than just a bare touch, his fingers reluctantly returning her clothes to decency.

Pulling back, he pressed the button on the key chain to unlock the doors.

"Get in," he said, hearing the unsteadiness of his voice.

Sharonda's gaze lingered for a moment longer on his lips before she slipped into the passenger seat. Taking off his jacket, James dropped it in the back seat, trying to calm his overeager hormones.

Then without a word, he took the driver's seat and simply drove. They made it through the mad traffic, then through several red lights.

"Long flight?" she asked cautiously, conversationally.

"Long enough."

She wiggled and partially reclined her seat. "Hard?"

He latched on to the innuendo. "Painfully so."

The jazz from the radio was a low strung melody, and if anything, it seemed to intensify the soft scratch of nylon when she crossed her legs.

"How was your day?" he asked, trying to remain polite.

"Wet. Storms are in the forecast."

He gripped the wheel and smiled, taking in the show. It started at a stop light, when her hand carelessly brushed off invisible lint and the trench coat parted, pulling apart to reveal the soft skin of her thigh. There the silk nylon tempted, held in place by a thin black satin ribbon that was woven into the top band then tied in a tiny delicate bow.

Hot damn! Right then and there, he promised himself he was going to undo that silly little bow with his teeth before the night was through.

He randomly took a left and followed the path onto the freeway. Somehow, an attempt to avoid a traffic jam led him to the outskirts of the city. By now the silence sank into the space between them, merging the light scent of his cologne with her perfume.

Peripherally, he saw her adjust the pearls at her neck, her fingers lingering, then moving slowly lower to undo a button that hid her breasts from view. He turned a bit to see the shirt sag open, just short of revealing her nipples.

"Umm, James?"

He looked straight ahead, then heeded her casual warning, correcting the fact that the car had started moving over the center divider.

A quick glance revealed her amusement; her lips curled into a lush smile.

He grinned.

They shared a hot look before she ran her hand in a stroking motion over the seat belt in a restless, distracting manner. Nice fingers. Long. And the way they moved, back and forth over the belt, the red tips of her nails—

"Keep your eyes on the road," she teased.

He did. Reluctantly.

She leaned closer, as if to point out something, but instead her hand landed on his chest, then played downward until she was slipping her hand over his erection, tugging down the zipper, working through the opening of his underwear to expose his full erection and hold it in her hand.

"Darling Sharonda, you're going to cause a crash!"

"Should I stop?"

The word yes simply refused to find its way to his mind,

much less his lips. He found he was gunning the engine and absently wondered when he'd driven this far out into the county.

Her hand moved expertly, stroking with familiarity. He glanced down occasionally, but even as he tried focusing on the road, his mind was crowded with the sight of her nimble fingers wrapped around him, just as he had fantasized.

Her thumb eased over his length, stroking, then rubbing the plum tip of his erection until he groaned from the pure pleasure.

"Sure would like to kiss it," she whispered.

He wasn't sure what he muttered, but he turned sharply to the first dusty road he came to, glad to find it isolated. He thanked his lucky stars when a short distance away, a small tunnel appeared. In the peaceful setting, the tunnel was at a crossroad, serving as a bridge for traffic crossing over the tunnel as well as for traffic going through it.

And yet, perfectly isolated.

Pulling up inside the tunnel, he yanked on the brakes and turned toward her. The truth was he was going to tell her she didn't have to do it. Because of what he'd read in her diary, he knew she didn't enjoy fellatio.

But her cheeks were flushed with arousal, her lips puffy and lush, her eyes hot with passion. The trench coat had fallen open, pulling on the cream-colored shirt, accentuating the lush cocoa dark brown of her skin, giving him almost an entire view of her full right breast. One glimpse of her nipple proved it looked as taut as his penis in her grasp.

"Lean back and enjoy," she said, reminding him of the similar words he'd said to her not too long ago.

James eased back, smiled and waited.

❧❧

Sharonda felt powerfully wicked. She unbuckled her seatbelt. Then his.

Reaching for his erection again, she stroked him in long, even strokes. He shifted, parting his thighs further so she could stroke his full length then come down to cup his testicles.

Sharonda marveled at the hot flesh in her grasp, at the way the hard roundness seemed to pulsate in her palm, the way it stretched upward, thick veined and solid. His male scent, reminding her of sex and lust, filled her nostrils. Had she really sworn off doing this when her mouth was practically watering now?

She leaned forward, the movement causing the pearls to drag against his thigh. With one breath she blew on him, and with the next, she licked the very tip of his phallus.

His hands curled to grip the seat and he stopped breathing.

Then because he tensed as if her touch was fire, she took

him completely into her mouth in a hungry suckle.

"Sss!"

It was delicious torment to try to wrap her tongue around him, then to stroke and slide the length of her lips on him, learning the rhythm of suction, the increase of oral tugging and trailing.

The sounds he made were barely marked grunts, his body so centered on what she did, that she deliberately stretched out each oral caress, gently rubbing the tightness of his testicles.

Jazz blended with breathlessness, until she could tell that his needs were becoming too much. His left hand moved to the base of her head, leading her more steadily.

She swallowed and licked, humming in appreciation.

"Sugar," he warning, his face tight and drawn.

The length of his penis got amazingly plump and his hand tightened in her hair. She stroked him eagerly, using mouth and hands until he came with a coarse cry, spilling his release deep in her mouth.

Sharonda swallowed the taste of his orgasm, lapping up any spillage until his body weakened. When she finally leaned back, her back ached from being in the curved position, but she was thoroughly and completely aroused.

James's chest rose and fell while he gathered his breath and composure. A soft sheen of sweat glistened from his brow. "Shhugaaar, you are something else."

His lips moved to form the slow, wicked smile she'd come to love. She made a show of licking her lips, then leaned forward to use the rear view mirror to check the lipstick that promised not to fade. Wow, it really hadn't faded. And she'd enjoyed that! Really enjoyed it.

"You damn near killed me," he said, his hand straying to her thigh and toying with the tiny bow on the nylon.

"I've been wanting to taste you there," she said, meaning it.

He looked genuinely pleased. "It's not fair to you though. Give me a minute to recover"

Sharonda felt the squeeze of his hand, barely moving from where he touched her thigh. Glancing outside, she noticed that the sun outside was fading quickly, coloring the sky in a picture perfect backdrop of lavender and gold. James handsome face was relaxed, but his eyes watchful.

With his eyes holding hers, he moved his hand from her thigh to the last restraining button of her shirt. As soon as it popped free, her breasts were revealed.

He admired them for a few seconds, and simply by that, they tightened even more.

Suddenly, he sat up, looking energized, and unlocked the doors. "Step outside."

She did and the gentle wind tugged at her coat.

"Come over here, honey," he said as he stood next to his door.

Her heels wobbled on the gravel, but she went to him,

grinning at the sight of him still in such formal suit, yet sporting a resurgent erection.

James placed her between himself and the car, his hands moving in a single stroke to pull the coat down her shoulders to where her butt leaned on the hood.

"The pearls are a nice touch," he said as she stood before him practically naked. "You should always wear jewelry."

His hands were on her hips as his head lowered to nudge the shirt aside and kiss the weak spot at her nape. Sharonda shivered. The nipples were just so sensitive as they brushed his shirt. He pushed her further backwards until her elbows touched the hood, the coat between her and the heat of the engine.

He took her breast between his lips, slipping his fingers past the wetness between her thighs and deep into her vagina, dragging a long moan from her as she arched her back.

"Mmmm..."

The wind took her words, mixing them with the ruffling of tree leaves beyond.

His fingers began to plunge in half-turns until she was soft, juicy wet and crazy with passion. She could only look dizzily at him when he abruptly stepped back as if to admire his handiwork.

"Perfect," he said. She imagined the picture she made, spread out on the shiny car hood, thighs apart to reveal her wetness, her breasts exposed, her cream colored shirt sagging around her. The silky black nylons, the white pearls and the hot red lipstick hid nothing else at all.

"Ditto," she replied. From where she was, he looked perfect too. His sleeves to his white shirt were rolled up, the belt and zipper of his trousers undone, and his cock loaded and ready. He looked like Mr. Banker turned into Mr. Sex Freak.

"Better than my fantasy," he complimented.

It warmed her to hear him say so. "Then how do you want it?" she taunted.

"Flip over," he said, low and even.

Enjoying the power he gave her, she flipped, going so far as to raise the tail end of her shirt for his view.

He grabbed his erection in his hand and stroked, then hurried to fit a condom on. He moved to stand behind her, ready to surge between her parted thighs. "Hard and fast, or slow and—"

"Hard and fast. Please."

His hands gripped her hips and he moved, inch by inch, into her saturated wetness, thrusting until he was deep into her welcoming cervix. Her breasts shifted against the heat of the coat, stimulating her nipples.

"Like that?" he asked between clenched teeth.

Absolutely!!!

There was no time to respond as he began to run his hands under her shirt, his nails lightly scratching her spine as he remained thick within her. He massaged her shoulders, giving one brief thrust of his hips, then moved his hands to her breasts, where her nipples were already overly sensitive. By the time his hands were on her wrists, his thrusts were getting firmer, shoving her against the hard body of the car with the force of his pumping.

Straight ahead, she could see the dimming sunset against the beautiful country road, and amid the riveting pleasure of the consuming sex, she couldn't help but feel naughty and exposed.

The friction mounted, shimmering in her gut, causing her to clutch the coat and brace for the orgasm she felt swelling with each thrust.

"Oh... James! Oh..."

He curved over her and squeezed his hand beneath her body to rub her clitoris. In the short uncompromising plunges that followed, she came like a firecracker, arching her back and pushing backwards into him to absorb as much of his rigid sex as possible while he rubbed and plunged and rubbed and plunged.

They both heard the far off sound of a car at the same time, but when she tried to jerk away, he pinned her where she was, his bold erection still threatening to ejaculate.

"James!"

"It's not this road," he said, panting hard.

When she glanced back, she knew he was right, but she still panicked. "They'll see us!"

"No, they won't." He remained rock hard and unmoving. Seconds passed this way, both of them trying to verify the direction of the unseen vehicle.

"It's not this road," he repeated.

She meant to agree, but he was suddenly moving again, pumping harder as the sounds of the car seemed to come closer.

"Oh my," she gasped, almost to the point of not caring. The noises of the approaching car engine became uncomfortably nearer.

The panic and thrill mixed, making her want to flee and yet she wanted to ride out the risk.

No sooner had she finished the thought than he shoved once, twice, compressing the last inch of his cock into her and ejaculating just as the traveling car moved over the tunnel above their heads. The echo of tires and gravel above muffled his harsh grunts of release, the heat of it starting her helpless and weaker vaginal contractions.

He crumpled onto her back and stayed that way until the sounds of the departing car faded into the distance.

"Told you they wouldn't see us," he mumbled.

"You are so crazy," she scolded weakly.

"Mmm. I know I should've stopped, but..." His hand caressed her spine under the shirt. The dimming light revealed that already most of the dusk was turning into night.

"But?"

"It was your round butt that had me going anyway."

Grinning hugely, she looked back at him. "We could've been caught! Right here!"

"But we weren't. And besides, you took the dare."

His smirk was just too cocky, but she loved it. "Yeah, guess so."

He kissed her briefly, his tongue flicking against hers. "It's getting dark. Ready to go?" he asked.

She nodded.

They separated, straightened their clothing and returned to their seats.

Halfway down the country road, on their way back to the city, Sharonda began to think of how embarrassing it would've been if they'd been caught. What could she have said? What could he? There would be no way to explain that one to her mother!

She glanced at James and caught his eye. Abruptly, she turned to look out the window, unable to hold back a chuckle.

James tried to hide his burst of laughter behind a cough, but when their eyes met again, their laughter was contagious, infectious.

Even after the chuckles had faded, Sharonda couldn't keep the smile from her lips.

Chapter 10

By the time they arrived at the apartment complex it was early night. As they stepped into the old elevator, James put his arm around her, waiting until elevator was between floors to press the stop button.

"What are you doing?"

"Trying out another one of my fantasies," he replied as he stood behind her. "Got a problem with that?"

"No." She caught his eye in the polished bronze interior that reflected their image like a mirror. They looked like a couple coming home from the corporate world.

Still keeping eye contact, his hands moved to undo the tie of her trench coat, then to unbutton her shirt, parting it to reveal her full breasts, her introverted navel, her trimmed pubic hair, and the delicate bows at her thighs that held the nylons in place.

"Every time I'm in here lately, I start thinking of this," he said, his hands moving in slow circles over her belly. The movements were possessive, almost hypnotic if not for the subtle hitch in his breathing. For restless minutes, all he did was take inventory of her with his eyes and the wide span of his hands, until those agile fingers began to dip toward her legs.

Sharonda shivered with warmth, widening her stance just a tad bit more for comfort. In the mirror, she watched him make a wanton stranger of herself while his fingers created a tide-lapping, relentless rhythm. The pearls gleamed when she turned her head, and he took it as an invitation to kiss her neck.

"What are you up to...?"

One of his hands cupped her left breast while his other hand slipped wetly out of her vagina to caress her aching clitoris. "Watching you simmer, babe. Nice and slow..."

Simmer. That was exactly how she felt. Maybe even a bit more than that. Maybe a hard boil. A burn.

Sharonda felt as if she'd drUnk too much wine. The tug of his hands drew on the fire curling in her gut, dragging a moan out of her that echoed erotically in the confines of the elevator.

She withstood the intimate caresses until her legs trembled and the need for more make her arch against his hand. Still breathing erratically, she turned in his embrace and kissed him, pushing her hips against his erection. There was nothing simmering about the kiss, just pure fire.

"I can simmer," she managed to say the moment they broke apart,

His pupils were a dark, intense brown, but a crooked smile

curved on his lips. "The question is, how much simmering can you handle, babe?"

She raised an eyebrow and tried to look calm, knowing she was probably falling far short from looking calm. "I can out-simmer you."

"Sounds like a challenge."

She licked her dry lips. "Did I mention that I'm flexible."

He groaned, his smile slipping. "Literally or figuratively?"

"Both, of course."

His eyelids half-closed and he groaned, making her feel sexy and just a bit immodest.

"Is it getting too hot for you?" she asked, running her index finger over his lips. She loved it that she could feel this daring, that he was drawn by it. It was thrilling to know she had his full attention with just her finger on his lip.

He bit into it gently, the sharpness of his teeth tempered by the lick of his warm tongue. He tugged the finger into his mouth and sucked on it, his eyes on hers. Deep in her gut the coils of desire were heating up even more.

Such a simple thing, and yet it was more seductive than any foreplay of her previous lovers. She bit her lip and swallowed to stifle any sound, then gently pulled her hand free.

"Can you take the heat?" he asked wickedly.

"Can you?" she countered, deciding to give him the same treatment. Taking his left hand, she pressed her lips to his palm, then traced a circle with her tongue and licked up to his

114

thumb, returning the love bite in the soft flesh of his thumb.

His breathing was deeper and his eyes blazed with contained fires. There was that split second when she was almost sure he'd give in, but he controlled his breathing and asked, "Is that the best you've got?"

"No. That was just a firecracker. Wait 'til I throw you a couple of grenades..."

"Hmmm... That's all talk."

"Like this here..." She raised her right leg to the hip high bar.

"Oh yeah..." He kissed her lustily, his hand following her thigh until he had her ankle in his grasp. "We'll have to explore this more."

That bad boy smile curved on his lips and he pressed the second floor button, bringing the elevator back to life. Stepping back a bit, he gave Sharonda just enough space for her to lower her leg, then hastily re-tie the trench coat.

When they exited, she followed the tug of his hand and went with him to his apartment. Finally, she thought with an awed sense of anticipation and apprehension. Finally, she was in his apartment! Not just dreaming about it. She was really in his home, playing a daring game of "simmer." A game she planned on winning!

As soon as the door closed behind her, he pinned her to the door and kept his mouth hovering with butterfly kisses on the arch of neck.

"I'd love to see you in rubies," he said, moving up to her jawline. "Nothing but rubies…"

"Maybe if I let you win, I might wear some." She felt his smile.

"Let me? Let me win?"

"Absolutely." She sucked in air when he nipped her skin.

"Hmm."

"Just trying to be fair, James. You're probably not as flexible as I am."

He left a scarf of kisses that trailed to her cleavage. "Maybe not, but I'd like to think I'm creative. Between you and me…"

Those clever hands were cupping her buttocks, his body held tightly against hers. The sound of his breath and the feel of him was delightful.

"Yes?" she gasped.

"Are you hot?" he teased. "Want to take something off?"

"No!"

The shrill of his phone rudely interrupted her thoughts. After the second ring the answering machine picked up. They both looked at each other, reluctant to part.

"Hey, Cooper! Did you forget it's poker night? It's your turn to bring the cigars, man. Henry over here says you've probably got your hands on some hottie," his friend laughed. "I say you're sitting on the toilet and clipping your toe nails. Well, dude, when you get this, give us a holler. I'm out."

The dial tone briefly sounded before it was silenced.

"What do you know," James drawled. "I do have a hottie in my hands!"

Flattered, but distracted, she held back the urge to slip her arms around him when he said, "I should call them back."

Like a burst bubble, she looked away to hide the sharp disappointment. "I didn't realize you had plans—"

"Just poker." Then he grinned. "And I still plan to. Poke her, that is… With you."

With sweet relief, she leveled her more deadpan gaze at him, "All I know is Crazy Eight."

"Poker's more fun. Allow me to teach you." His hands squeezed her butt.

"You are such a lech!"

The phone rang again. He sighed.

"Go ahead and take the call," she said, easing away from the door.

He nodded and with his erection pushing at his zipper, he walked over to the phone and answered it.

"Hello… What's up, Henry."

Sharonda moved around the room, trying to give him some privacy, yet all the while feeling the heat of his gaze on her spine. Exhaling carefully, she lectured herself while admiring a beautiful Nigerian mask. This was turning out to be another magical night! She could hear him canceling with his friends to stay with her.

She would have this. One more night of fantasies. His. Or hers.

"Simmer" really was his fantasy. And there was no way she was going to lose. She could do this. Although losing wasn't going to be a bad deal either.

Sharonda turned to face him and found that he was still talking on the phone. But his eyes were steadily on her.

As if she were starring in a porn film, she let her fingers undo the tie of her trench coat then slipped it off in the sexiest way possible. Her shoulders barely shimmied, allowing the material to slip off. Then after laying it on his couch, she began doing up a few buttons to her shirt.

James never once blinked, but his responses had become almost rude ah-huhs. After a pause, he opened a box of cigars nearby and held one up to her.

Strolling to him on the tall heels, she accepted the cigar, putting it under her nose and inhaling the luxuriant leafy scent the way she imagined the experts did. Then holding it with her finger tips, she put it between her lips, feeling the return of power when his eyes focused on her lips holding the thick cigar.

"Henry, I gotta go. Talk to you later." James hung up the phone without delay. "You like cigars?"

"Never had one."

"I don't smoke 'em. They're just for bluffing during poker."

118

She pretended to suck on the cigar as if it was lit, smiling when his nostrils flared as if he remembered just what the pull of suction felt like.

"I believe I owe you a lesson or two? Are you up for it?" he asked.

"Sure. I can take your money."

He chuckled, low and sexy, a devil tickled by an angel's feather. "But we're not playing for money, shug. We're playing for stripping rights."

"Oh?" She watched him pick up a deck of cards lying next to the cigars.

"Yes. The rules can be simple. I'll pick a card, you pick a card and the one with the highest rank gets to strip one single item of clothing from the other. Winner gets a final wish."

Sharonda felt her blood thicken with excitement. "Not fair, you have more clothes than I do. You should remove two items of clothing instead of one."

His grin was full of charm and underhanded intent. "Deal."

"And no cheating."

"Me cheat?" he asked with amazing innocence. "But just so you know, I can beat you at this, and still out-simmer you."

Simmering was for wimps! She was going to win! "So quit talking and let's play," she challenged.

He touched the pearls at her throat, faintly adjusting them. Sharonda forced herself to quell the instinctive urge to lean into his hand.

James smiled and Sharonda had the feeling she'd been suckered. But the night was still young, still brimming with opportunity.

The first game was his and by the way he whipped the card around, she was almost sure he'd cheated. Smooth jazz was wallowing from the speakers when he raised his eight of diamonds, defeating her three of spades.

Ah, hell!

He looked her over, letting his eyes travel from her head down to the slightly parted shirt, then her clad legs, down to the high-heeled shoes.

"What will it be?" she asked huskily, pretending to nonchalantly flick cigar ash. Already her gut was in warm knots of anticipation.

"The earrings," he said.

"Ah-ah. You only get one, not both."

"I forgot," he said although his eyes revealed the lie. In a predatory move, he stood to walk the single step and lean over her, lowering his head until his breath brushed her cheek. Then with his lips, he worked the clip-on earring from her ear lobe, nuzzling and kissing the soft skin below her ear until she moaned.

Victorious, he sat back in his seat and placed the token win on the table.

"Next," he said, indicating she should take a card from the stack.

Again his card beat hers and his chuckle was downright triumphant. "Better luck next time," he mocked as he approached her to begin the oral removal of the other earring.

She was so tempted to touch him, she had to grip the armrest to keep from holding his lips where they were. He took more time nuzzling her pulse than removing her earring. Man, he had such a wicked tongue!

"Just say the word, babe, and the game is over," he whispered.

Despite the urge to concede, she licked her dry lips and said, "Are you forfeiting?"

He moved his face until he could see into her eyes. "No."

Up close she could see all the rough and manly textures of his skin. "Then... I guess we play until you beg for mercy."

A smile barely reached his lips, but the depths of his eyes registered humor. "Big talk for someone who hasn't even won one round."

His mouth was so near, the urge to kiss him expanded. Just once. Damn, why did he have to lick his lips like that? Before she could make up her mind, he moved back to his chair.

This time when they drew cards, her king beat his six.

"I get two items," she rushed to say, the excitement clear in her voice.

He seemed ready for her. "Go for it."

Trying to appear as confident as he had earlier, she took her time looking him over, pausing a few seconds more than necessary at his crotch.

"Well?"

"I think it'll be your belt and your underwear," she said.

"Wait, you can't do that," he complained. "My pants have to come off first and then my underwear."

"No, no," she said, casually waving about the unlit cigar. "You said two items of clothing. You didn't say there was an order as to how they come off."

He looked so handsome sitting there, sporting a hard on and silently acknowledging her point with a shrug.

"Stand up," she commanded.

He stood and she knelt before him. Then taking every chance to brush her body against his, she fumbled with his belt. It came off slowly, a hiss of leather, followed by the sound of his zipper being lowered. After cupping his buttocks in her hands, she began pulling the trousers downwards until they brushed her shirt and finally pooled around his ankles.

His erection, only inches from her face, seemed amazingly uncomfortable in his briefs. Oh, the smells of sex! She exhaled, letting her breath blow over the briefs. "Just say the word, James, and the game is over. I'll even stay right where

I am," she said, catching the burst of temptation in the depths of his eyes.

"I don't think so. But keep the position in mind for later—"

The mere touch of her breasts against his legs silenced him. It was either that or the fact that she'd started to remove his briefs, letting her teeth tug at the elastic band, working gently and as tantalizingly as possible to release his erection from the tight confines.

When she could hardly manage any more, she used her hands to lower his briefs to his ankles. She resisted touching him again, but smiled in satisfaction when he sat back down, his breaths deep, pushing against his shirt.

"I want to double the odds," he said huskily. "If my card beats yours, I get to take off two items of your clothing, and you can take off four of mine."

Four! Why, they'd be naked in no time! "All right."

He dealt each of them a card in another one of his fast-wrist moves.

On unsteady legs, she sat back down and turned her card over. A seven.

The following silence was so intense, it seemed to drown out the saxophone blues. Their eyes locked, but she would've sworn he looked like he already knew the outcome, which meant that he might have cheated.

He turned his card over.

Delilah Dawson

"Damn," she murmured when the card face revealed a ten. "The nylons."

She should've known.

"Here's a taste of your own medicine," he said as he knelt before her to remove them. She'd had his mouth on her thighs before, but this time, his intentions were to torture her without actually getting anywhere near her sex. Copying the way she'd removed his underwear, he got to work.

He undid the bows with his teeth, then tugged the individual nylons down her thighs, pausing to use his hands to remove them from her shoes and off her legs.

It seemed like a lifetime before he went back to his chair, wasting precious time by starring longingly at her before dealing the next set of cards.

"Necklace and shirt," he said when he won again.

"You're cheating!"

"Prove it."

She huffed but failed to hide her smile.

"Now, don't be a sore loser, babe," he knelt between her thighs, burying his head between her breasts.

"I demand a rematch," she said huskily, even as he removed the shirt from her body.

"Oh, yeah..."

The necklace came off with a flick of his wrist.

His breath was warm as it blew over her skin. "But right this minute, it looks like I won," he teased, still watching her,

124

his tongue flicking over her left nipple. "Who's begging for mercy now?"

Not one to throw in the towel, Sharonda replied, "Game's not over yet."

He licked the nipple again, then sucked it until she found herself holding her breath.

"I get a wish, remember?" he reminded her as he moved on to her other breast.

Sharonda tried to loosen her grip on the armrests. "Mmm-hmm."

Her breasts, already plump with arousal, yearned for the stimulation of his mouth. "So, what's your wish?" she managed to ask between breaths.

He paused to look at her and for a minute it seemed as if he were battling himself. Finally he said, "For you to be my shower slave."

"A shower slave? As in to take a shower?"

His lips twitched into a smile. "Yeah."

Oh, this was too easy! All she had to do was lather him up and stroke him the right way—

"Well?"

"Okay..."

Naked, he led her into his bathroom, turned on the water in the tiny shower stall. With a backwards step, he tugged her into the stream of water with him. When the door closed, the space seemed smaller, his wide shoulders seeming to hog the room

Without a word, he handed her a small washcloth and a bottle of masculine scented liquid soap. As the water drizzled down on them, she soaped up the washcloth until the lather was rich and foamy. She hadn't touched him and yet his penis was as hard and stiff, straining toward her.

Water played lightly on his shoulders, drizzling slightly onto her as she placed the washcloth square against his chest. With their eyes locked in a steady gaze, she began to clean him, every inch of his chest, his hips, then his hardened and eager cock.

His eyes grew heavy-lidded, and he leaned forward, bracing an arm on either side of her, making her wonder if he was worried his knees would give.

"Getting too hot for you?" she asked, barely turning down the hot water knob. She brushed her lips against his jaw, her nipples pushing against his soft chest hair.

His eyes narrowed and with his smile fixed firmly in place, he turned around. "You forgot to scrub my back."

More of the hot water sprayed on her as he moved, the touch of liquid searing her gently, sucking her breath away with steam, the way his kisses could. Lord, she hoped he'd give in soon!

He looked at her over his shoulder, then turned away, as if preparing himself for the worse.

So she gave it to him. Alternating between the use of her

hands and body, and the utility of the washcloth, she scrubbed his gorgeous back. Her fingers splayed over the breadth of his shoulders, his muscular spine. She watched the soapy bubbles wash away, grazing her body on the way down.

Then placing her hands on the flanks of his buttocks, she placed a kiss between his shoulder blades, feeling light-headed with deprived need, too much steam and oversexed hormones.

Wrapping her arms around him, she cupped his penis and stroked, relishing his broken moan and lowered head. "Christ!"

"Do you give up?" she asked.

His hand clamped over hers, pausing the torture. His swallow was loud, but he said, "No. But maybe you will."

Turning around, he grabbed the washcloth, lathered it back up and placed it against her navel, saying, "My turn."

"Wait just a minute, I..."

The cloth swirled right, dipping toward her pubic hair then coming back up to touch the bottom of her breasts.

"You what?" he asked, seeing her wordless response.

"Hmm?"

He was focused on completely washing her breasts, making sure the texture rubbed back and forth over the sensitive nipples, leaving her no choice but to close her eyes and try to control her breathing. It was little relief to know she wasn't the only one trying to stay in control.

"You could... give in." he said gruffly.

"No... way..."

The washcloth in his hand moved south, between the delta of her thighs.

"James! ... Not fair..."

The washcloth was dropped, his hand taking its place.

"Oh..." She leaned into him, wanting... wanting...

"Give in, babe."

She bit her bottom lip before words betrayed her. Then rolling her forehead against his chest, she simmered hard while his fingers plunged in deeper. Hungrily, she turned her mouth to his water-slicked chest and sank a love bite there. His fingers momentarily stilled, his breath blew hard against her temple.

"Don't you want me inside you?" he asked.

Yes! Yes! God, YES!

When her lips almost touched his, she slid her hand over his erection. He quivered against the contact. "Do you want to be inside me?" she countered. "I'm so ready for you, babe..." She stroked him, and his hand that reached to stop her weakened. "James, all you have to do is...give in."

"Sharondaahh... Yes," he said roughly, grabbing her and lifting her against his chest. His mouth slanted over hers as he hoisted her higher then lowered her, sheathing himself into her slick vagina, all the way to the hilt.

There was no room for words; breath and moans seemed

lost in the warm mist. The moment became frozen in that intimate embrace where she clung to him under a stream of water that seemed to seal limbs and mouths and sexes. Like statues. Not leaning on anything at all.

The first two thrusts were tiny, more like the shift of earth settling after a quake. And yet the effect was hard enough to send her mind wobbling, reeling, jazzing such a violent orgasm that it shook through her like a whip.

James lost his balance but recovered when his back hit the wall. Not even stunned, he braced his legs and surged into her, pumping hard, finding release within seconds.

Weak-limbed, they clung together for what felt like an eternity.

When the water began to turn cold against her spine, she reached up and turned it off. Water trickled noisily down the drain and James huffed in air like a wounded beast.

Weak but triumphant, she too sucked in air, then muttered, "I won!"

Chapter 11

Time flowed into days, where it seemed as if her every thought was consumed by James. Then for two days, his grandfather decided to spend most of the night playing dominoes with him. It was frustrating that she couldn't call him or even set the wind chimes out.

On the third day, they fell into his bed lustily, grappling and striving for satisfaction of the rawest urge to copulate.

It was much later, somewhere between night and a premature dawn, when Sharonda realized there was nothing more comforting than the cocoon of toasty warm flannel sheets, her sleeping lover's chest hair tickling her nose and the utter feeling of rightness. Mentally coasting somewhere between being completely asleep and partially awake, she thought it just had to be heaven.

The pristine moment was shattered by the rude shrill of the phone. Sharonda's first reaction was to automatically reach for the unit. James merely turned his head as if the sound had been a mosquito buzzing nearby.

"Hello?" she asked groggily.

"Oh! Umm, is James there?"

Old Man Cooper! Sitting straight up, she poked at James, whispering threats so he would wake up. His eyes cracked open, then promptly slid shut. It took tweaking his chest hair to get his attention.

"What?" he grumbled.

She pointed madly at the phone.

James frowned, sighed, put the phone to his ear and closed his eyes, his words slurring slightly. "James here."

Clutching the bed sheet to her chest, she tried to make out the conversation muffled by his pillow.

"Yeah. Right now?" He glanced at the alarm clock. Can it wait? Oh. "Well, okay, Gramps I'll be there in a few. Un-huh. Goodbye."

James hung up the phone, then peered at Sharonda through half-drooped eyelids, as if he couldn't quite remain awake. He absently rubbed his chest where she'd tweaked his hair. "Sugar?"

The endearment nestled warmly in her chest. "Hmm?"

"Duty calls. I'm going to Mr. Hoskin's apartment for just a bit. Gramps says the pipe is leaking badly and water's everywhere."

She wondered how the magic could be snuffed out so quickly when just minutes ago everything had seemed so perfect. "Do you want me to leave?"

"No. I should be back soon." He rubbed his eyes as he turned to sit, pulling her, sheets and all, onto his lap. "Next time take it easy on my chest hair, okay?"

"I'm sorry. I picked up the phone without thinking, then I panicked," she admitted, accepting the kiss he placed on her cheek before putting her back on the bed. "No offense to your grandfather, but he does like to gossip a bit and if my mother gets wind of this—"

"Believe me, I know." James stepped into the bathroom, his voice distanced by the sound of running water as he quickly washed his face and brushed his teeth. "I doubt he heard enough of your voice to figure out who you are."

When he returned he was buttoning up his jeans and pulling on a t-shirt.

"It's just that if he said anything to my mother, she's bound to jump to conclusions," she hurried to explain.

He smiled widely while putting on his sneakers. "Wrong ones?"

"You know what I mean."

"Yes." His eyes locked with hers, filled with understanding. The words 'matchmaking hell' didn't need to be said aloud, nor did she need to spell out her fears about the intense meddlesome strategies her mother could invent.

"I'll be back soon," he said, laying a brief toothpaste-scented kiss on her lips.

"James, I think I'll head back to my place and get ready for work. But maybe we can get together for dinner?"

He twirled his keys in his hand. "Wouldn't you rather

stay?"

"Yes, but you don't have a blow drier and... stuff."

"Oh."

Running a large palm over his scratchy beard, he eyed her cleavage, then returned, standing too close to her.

"Should you be going?" she asked, firming her grip on the sheet.

"Hmm. Yes. I should." He tugged on the flannel covering her.

"Jaammesss."

"I'm going, I'm going."

She slapped his hand before he completely pulled the sheet off.

"Spoilsport," he accused, then winked at her before heading out the door.

Days later, Sharonda was in the process of unlocking her door when she heard a jingle-jangle from down the hall. Turning her head, she saw James sauntering her way, a pipe wrench in one of his gloved hands while the other kept a flashlight on his tool belt from knocking against his thigh.

"Hey there, Ms. Williams," he said politely.

She smiled and inclined her head. "Mr. Cooper." After looking down both sides of the hallway she let her eyes linger over him, taking in the handyman stained t-shirt, the old, almost white, jeans and finally with much relish, the entire male package that was intimately and exclusively hers.

His eyes warmed under the scrutiny. "Ah, was that you that called about needing some adjustment to your plumbing?" He lowered his voice to a whisper. "I think you mentioned a gradual leak?"

She glanced at his tool belt, then below to his zipper. "If you've got the right tool, we could get to work right away."

"Well, ma'am, I aim to please."

From down the hall, the elevator doors binged open and Sharonda stiffened guiltily, her smile weakening when she spotted Old Man Cooper stepping out of the elevator and heading in their direction.

Eyes twinkling and leaning heavily on his cane, the elderly man flashed his wide smile in greeting.

"Hey, kids. What's going on?"

Sharonda returned the smile, but worked on getting her key in the lock. It was important to make things appear to be platonic. Surely they could make him think she'd just needed James handyman assistance for a few minutes. If he thought there was more to it, he'd call her mother. And besides, if her mother caught wind of the slightest romantic inclination, she'd be in a flurry of matchmaking all over again.

James greeted his grandfather with a familiar pat on the back. "Hey Gramps."

"So what's going on?" Old Man Cooper repeated.

"Ms. Williams was saying she has a slow leak under the kitchen sink, so I was letting her know that if she had the time now, I could take a look at it."

Sharonda concentrated on getting the door open, hoping her face wouldn't betray the blush she felt clear to her bones.

"Thought that plumbing was pretty new," Old Man Cooper said with a thread of concern.

"Oh, it's probably a minor thing," James assured him. "In any case, I'm sure it's something I can fix."

Sharonda sighed quietly in relief when the door was finally unlocked.

"Good. Good," the old man said. Then when Sharonda turned back toward them, he asked, "And how's that cold doing?"

She frowned. "Cold?"

"Remember the other day when I made the delivery? You said you were catching a cold or something."

"Ohhh, yes. Well, that's gone. Yes, I took some medicine and the symptoms disappeared."

Above the old man's head, Sharonda caught the wink James sent her way.

A brief moment of silence followed the remarks of "Good. Good."

"How're you doing?" she inquired, trying at being social.

"Doing good. This old leg of mine needs therapy so I've

taken to walking and that seems to help a bit. Last time I talked to your mother, she promised to bring her famous Bundt cake next time she comes around."

James' smile became just a tad bit stiffer and Sharonda had to work to keep hers in place. Bundt cake? Long walks? What was this man hinting?

"You cook?" the old man asked with a hopeful glint in his eye.

"No. Not much," she hedged. "Nothing like my momma."

He shook his head as if she'd admitted to losing a limb. "Life's tough on women these days. Don't have time to cook and learn the old ways of soul food." Then as if realizing what he'd said he amended, "James knows how to cook. Boy knows how to do everything, but he sure can cook. Maybe y'all can get together, swap recipes and such."

And such?

Having been left out of the conversation thus far, James straightened, sending his tool belt creaking and the tools clinking gently together. "Guess I ought to take a look at the leaky pipes, if she can spare a few minutes."

Picking up her cue, Sharonda opened the door wider. "Yes, certainly. The kitchen is right through there. What am I saying? Of course you know where the kitchen is. I mean, since all the apartments are alike and all."

Old Man Cooper simply smiled as if he'd provided a service, stroked his goatee and then with a single tap of his cane on the floor, he said, "Well, you take care now. I'll see you kids later."

As soon as the door closed, securing their privacy, James wiggled his eyebrows and made a grab for her, frisking her as if to touch her everywhere at once, settling on the curves of her hips.

"James!" she scolded, covering her mouth with her hand in order to muffle her laughter.

With his hands around her, sliding to cup her buttocks, he half-dragged, half-carried her to the kitchen, all the while his mouth left kisses and the breath of his chuckles against her skin.

Finally pinned against the kitchen sink, Sharonda locked her fingers behind his neck. "A leak? Is that all you could think of saying?"

"I didn't hear you offering a better plan," he countered smugly, still nuzzling her ear. His hands went to her hips, his own hips positioned invitingly against hers.

"You could've said the, uh." She faltered, unable to think from the way he was licking the sensitive spot below her ear.

"Uh, what?"

"The, ummm, the thingie."

"Thingie? That wouldn't fly." His teeth sank into her neck like a vampire but it turned into another sensual kiss. "Thingie's getting hard," he whispered.

Delilah Dawson

"I know. I just meant he sounds like he knows—"

"He's just guessing." He never stopped with the butterfly kisses.

"Accurately," Sharonda mumbled, eyes half closed.

"He's meddling. Forget him. Our secret is safe."

Sharonda ignored the tiny dip in her gut. How would James feel if they were caught red-handed? Would their secret break their relationship? "James, what if... "

"Hmmm?"

His hands moved with familiarity under her shirt. When had he undone the buttons?

"I was just wondering..." Her fingers found the buckle of his belt.

"No talking," he murmured, his lips by her chin. "I'm busy trying to find a wet spot... Got a leak to fix... A hole to plug..."

The light wool skirt she wore made a rustling sound as it was gathered by his industrious fingers. His tool belt clinked again as he adjusted to slip his hand under the control top of her nylons. "Hmm, what tool should I use?"

"Are you going to keep with the puns," she asked, feeling lightheaded and biting back a chuckle.

Pretending to be affronted, he stopped nibbling just long enough to say, "You bet, baby."

Her laughter melted in the kiss he gave her. When they broke apart, breathing heavily, he asked, "Wanna go to the bedroom?"

"I, ah, I cleaned the kitchen last night."

"Hmm, that's good, but— Oh, the floor? The clean floor! Well then, let me start. I think I have an idea where the spouting is occurring..."

True to his word, he kept a constant commentary filled with sexual innuendo, about tools, pipe leaks and the arduous, necessary work of a plumber.

Between the taste of kisses, trembling flesh and passion they began slipping from the kitchen counter and ending up making hot and heavy love on the clean kitchen floor.

Chapter 12

The days at work dragged for Sharonda, but the nights were incredible. James. He was in every other thought, in every other sigh. The work hours seemed to clog together, the minutes rustling each second until the moment she could finally come home.

It was the melody of both their chimes, one from her balcony, one from his, that now welcomed her as soon as she stepped out of her car.

She was about to enter the building when she heard the guttural throttle of a motorcycle as it zoomed into a parking spot near the door. Black jeans hugged firm legs, a tobacco brown leather bomber jacket covered the torso and a tinted black helmet covered the man's face from view. But she knew it was James even before he flipped the visor upward.

A warm proprietary emotion spread in her chest as she watched him park his bike and approach in his long-legged stride, his helmet under one arm.

"Playing doorman?" he asked with a smile.

"Only for you."

He held the door instead. "No, no. After you."

Passing by him, she reached up and placed a kiss on his cheek. "Thanks."

"Once a boy scout..."

"Always a boy scout?"

"Yup. Remind me to show you my patches later."

"Is that like etchings?"

"Only better. I can provide demonstrations of competence. I got really high marks on some of them."

Her blood heated under his gaze as possibilities formed in her head. "Interesting."

They reached the elevators and pressed the call button. "I was wondering... How about going out for dinner tonight? Or better yet, a spontaneous weekend."

A weekend?! She glanced at him, trying to hold off the hopeful sensation that their relationship was becoming more personal than sexual. If only...

"Sounds good, I'll just need to change."

"Wear something casual, but warm. Jeans if you have them."

"Jeans?"

"And overnight clothes. You're not scared to ride motorcycles, are you?"

"No, but—"

"Cool." He pressed a button and the elevator ascended. "I have an extra helmet."

It was with a small amount of amazement that Sharonda found herself clinging to James' broad torso while the world whirled by in a blur of sunset colors. The turbo growl of the powerful motorcycle sent vibrations through her body. The wind was so clipped and cool, she could no longer smell the male scent of James in the leather jacket he'd bundled her in.

It had taken at least ten minutes from the moment he'd jetted from the parking lot for her to unclench her teeth, open her eyes and peer at the view. Like some sort of time travel, she watched the contours of buildings, cars and people give way with the passing miles to lush green trees and uncultivated land.

She loved it that James could just pick up and spontaneously do what he wanted. It was a bit overwhelming to know that his fantasies were realized on the fly. What would she have to do to make this weekend memorable?

Pulsing to a slow rhythm, dusk seemed to dance at the spiked tips of the trees, and as the miles gave way to deeper landscapes, Sharonda realized they were heading toward the ocean. The sky began turning Buddhist orange, then faded into a hazy purple sheen that quietly seduced the sun into the horizon. Soundlessly, she found the echo of rhythm in the ebb and flow of waves as they curled, eager to reach shores.

The smell of ocean reached her nose, and as the sun slowly surrendered to darkness, she clung to James, feeling safe and memorizing every moment.

Then night came. The throttle of the engine accompanied the darkness, her view becoming restricted to miserly moonlight, the headlight of the bike or any passing vehicles. Trees became obscure black lines and the ocean looked like a silver sequined scarf billowing under a soft wind.

Magical.

Finally, James pulled into a small town nestled on craggy cliffs that overlooked the horizon-wide ocean.

Her limbs still hummed with the phantom throb of the engine when James parked and they dismounted. After removing her helmet, she checked her hair, tucking in any stray strands and using the rear view mirror to check her make-up.

"Nice place," she commented, looking at the small restaurant. Even in the dim light she could see the worn exposed wood that had withstood the ocean's elements. Inside, the tables were covered with red and white plaid tablecloths and intimate candle settings. James held her hand in his. Sharonda felt as if her heart were beating in the flat of her palm, making a delicate tattoo against his hand.

The man who warmly greeted James had a walrus type moustache and a heavy New York accent. In a slightly exuberant fashion, they were led to a corner table where the man detailed the menu for her.

"I would suggest the crab special," James said in a stage whisper.

She agreed.

"Crab it is," the man said, scribbling away on his notepad. "And you're having the usual, James?"

"You know it."

"Good choice." With a flick of a lighter, the man lit the candle at the center of the table and made a discreet retreat.

"The usual?" she asked, suddenly wondering how often he ate at the restaurant.

"Scallops, fish and shrimp in wine sauce and capers. Very good, but so is the crab."

"Ah." She straightened her silverware to avoid his eyes, working to stem the surge of jealousy that flashed out of nowhere. How many women had he brought here?

James stretched out his hand on the table and after working up a smile, she placed her hand in his. He looked so handsome in the candlelight, her heart squeezed.

"You should see this place in the daylight," James said with enthusiasm. "The ocean goes on forever and you can see the fishing boats scattered all over the bay." His thumb grazed her knuckles. "If you don't get seasick, we can rent a boat and cruise around the bay tomorrow."

"Sounds wonderful." She tried not to dwell on the pesky jealousy that refused to be smothered.

"You'll see for yourself," he said. "I booked us a room at

the hotel down the street." Although her smile was enthusiastic, he wasn't fooled by it and the gleam in his eyes dimmed. "What's wrong?"

"Nothing."

He gave her fingers a squeeze, speaking quietly. "We're beyond that. Come on, tell me."

Shrugging to make little of it, she said, "I just wondered how often you came here."

He watched her intently while his thumb grazed her fingers again. "And?"

It wasn't fair to tell him, Sharonda told herself. Since the beginning, they'd never made promises for more than just sex. So she said, "Seems like a long way to drive for seafood... but I'm sure it's worth it."

He didn't look away. Instead he leaned forward and lifted her fingers to his lips. "The food is out of this world and that alone is worth the trip. Amazingly enough, I tend to come here alone. But every once in a while, I'll drive Gramps up for a relaxing weekend. Sharonda, I've never brought a woman here."

Her heart felt as if it clogged her throat. "I didn't ask."

"Not out loud."

With a sigh, she briefly touched the tines of her fork, then looked at him. "Okay, so I was curious. Forget I said anything okay? Tell me more about the bay."

His enigmatic eyes bored into her, interrupted only by the

timely appearance of a waiter who served their cashew-topped salads and chilled white wine.

When the waiter left, James wordlessly raised a toast, clinking his wineglass with hers. After a few sips, he began telling her more about his love for the bay.

❦

The wine was getting to her. James could tell by the sassy way she'd started to giggle when he said something funny. Maybe it was more than that. He hadn't expected her to wear the tight black tank top and black jeans with the chic boots. The only thing that kept her from looking completely the sensual wild creature was her hair, carefully bound up in a neat coiffure.

Testing her inhibitions, he said, "Let your hair down."

Sharonda wagged her finger at him and giggled. Man, that husky sound was powerful. It was nothing like a schoolgirl and everything like a seductress.

"My hair would be a mess," she complained. "How would it look when all the customers start screaming and running out of here because of me."

"Come on, do it for me," he coaxed. "Let it down."

"Are you serious?"

"Yes."

She took a long sip of wine to think it over, her eyes

reflecting the soft candlelight.

"Give me a minute and I'll be back," she said before standing and heading to the ladies' restroom.

When she returned, her hair was indeed down in an artful finger-combed fashion, her lipstick was refreshed and her mouth was curved into a wide, appealing smile that carried a hint of embarrassment and self-awareness.

"Gorgeous. I am the luckiest man in the place."

"Thank you." Another sip of wine followed while she played with the thin gold chain that hung down to her cleavage.

The reply James planned to make vanished when he felt spellbound, watching her pick up a breadstick and take a bite. Her teeth sank into it, her tongue licking any remaining crumbs from her lips. Knowing it was deliberate and loving the boldness, he visually tracked the nimble tongue until it slipped back into her mouth.

"Looks yummy," he commented.

"It is… Yummy… Here, taste it." She raised the remainder of the bread to his lips.

He took a bite and chewed, his eyes locked with hers over the flickering candle flame. When the tightness of his erection became too painful, he leaned back in his chair in an attempt to ease the eager pressure. Damned if she didn't smile like she knew it too. Discreetly, he looked around, glad that he'd been seated in an intimate corner of the restaurant.

The main course was served with the cool discretion of waiters who knew when to mind their own business.

"Mmm, don't you just love crab?" she asked, dipping the strip of white meat into the melted butter and eating it. This time, he was positive she wasn't being deliberate, and still it was sexy as hell. He covered up his half-groan with a cough. For the sake of the approaching waiter, he checked his clock and cleared his throat.

The waiter came and went, but Sharonda was undeterred.

It was no longer enough to just lean back to relieve the pain in his jeans, so he undid one button of his button fly, thankful that the table cloth hung well over his lap and all the way to the floor.

At some point, between the discussion of recent movies and favorite songs, dessert was served. With her cheeks flushed, Sharonda leaned forward as if for her purse. He heard the quiet zipper sound and when she leaned back, he assumed she had simply retrieved something from her purse.

The feel of her socked foot moving up his calf to his knee, then to his thigh, took him completely by surprise. The spoonful of pineapple sorbet remained an inch from his lips, his body bracing for the utter delight of her foot finding its way to his lap.

The sock was still warm from her boot and he instinctively nudged against it, holding her foot where the throbbing of his erection was the worst. God, he wanted her.

The lovesick mandolin melody was fading into the background when Sharonda licked the sorbet from her spoon. With deviant skill, she sucked the round end of the spoon into her mouth, her cheeks pulling taut at the action. The spoon slipped out clean from between her full lips and the whole process began again with another spoonful.

"Want some?" she offered in a husky whisper.

"Oh, I want all right. But not that." God, he damn near sounded like a teenager. Desperate. Horny. And he felt it too.

Willing himself to take control, he watched every spoonful until the dish was empty.

"You know," he said, when she smiled at him like a Cheshire cat, "I think I'll take some of that to go. Are you ready to see the room I booked?"

Chapter 13

Sharonda bit back a groan, trying to keep her hand on the iron wrought headboard the way James had told her to. The ceiling blurred in her vision as a true cold shiver snaked up her spine. How could something so insanely cold feel so good?!

"Oh, James, that's cooooollddd!" she mumbled weakly.

"Hush," he commanded. "Think of it as your bondage fantasy. Page one twenty-six?" He took a moment to readjust the pillows he'd placed under her butt to elevate her for his pleasure. With the spoon he placed another dollop of the flavorful sorbet between her spread legs, letting the instant heat cause a trickle to melt to her mons. Then lowering his head, he began to lick and eat the melting ice cream off her body, his tongue rubbing the tiny ice crystals into her sensitive nub and vaginal folds before licking it off. The roll of his tongue and the miniscule granular quality of the dessert was an entirely new texture that was driving her mad.

Her arms strained from holding the headboard, her back instinctively arching, the oral torture wringing a whimper from her.

When her focus returned, her face was turned to the clock

alarm on the bedside table.

"Twenty-three minutes more," he said against her skin, as if reading her mind.

James had concluded that she'd fondled his penis with her foot for thirty-four minutes, so he deserved the same amount of time on her.

His tongue plunged into her vaginal passage, cold limber tongue, warm greedy mouth.

"Oh!"

It was as if he'd made a meal of it, one that made her almost forget to keep gripping the headboard. Releasing the ironwork would mean to start over. And dammit she'd done that twice already!

The ice cream sitting on her nipples melted down the sides of her breasts in a cool trail. More was pooling in her belly button, waiting for him to get around to sipping it. But his attention never wavered, even when the orgasm that was whittled from her soul made her forget to keep her hands in place.

In the aftermath, she felt incredibly sublime and at peace, letting him lick the rest of the melted spots at his leisure. When he was ready, she lay in the tangled sheets and smiled to welcome him as he crawled over her body, feeling a wonderful passive pleasure even as he took his release from her tired and limp body.

James awoke to watch Sharonda sleeping. Lovers could do things like that, right? They could take each other out for the weekends, have mad sex and still want to watch every sleeping breath. Sure. Right.

With his finger, he rimmed the sheet where it covered one of her lovely breasts and left the other bare.

Fascinating. She was becoming too fascinating. Uninhibited. Delicious. And that was dangerous because he was getting involved. Really involved. If he were to tell her she was his best lover to date, he wondered how she would react. Would she believe that her innocence and eagerness were an incredible turn on?

But the reason he'd woken up plagued him again. He was starting to want her more than just in his bed.

Reaching to the bedside table, he clicked on the lamp, bringing on a soft light that dispelled the gray-black darkness of pre-dawn.

Blowing gently on the exposed nipple, he said her name gently, trying to wake her up. The nipple puckered to a cold tip, but Sharonda only frowned in her sleep. Man, he'd never met anyone who liked to sleep so much. Taking stronger measures, he lowered his head and suckled on the cold tip. Her frown disappeared into a low, moaned hum that stemmed from deep in her chest.

"Wake up, sleepy face," he coaxed.

"You're insatiable," she mumbled, slurring the words as she rolled over to cuddle up to his chest. "Let me sleep, pleaasssee."

He chuckled and palmed her butt, his erection starting to engage at the feel of her hips against his. "I want to show you something, but you gotta wake up. No sex. Promise."

She peered through one eye, her look letting him know he'd just eliminated the only single reason she would wake up.

"Guess I'll have to do things the hard way." In a flourish, he yanked the sheets toward the end of the bed. The cold air nipped her immediately.

"James!!!!" she shrieked, sounding as if she were out for blood.

He chuckled and barely dodged the pillow thrown at his head.

"I'm going to have to kill you," she threatened, sounding for the entire world as if she was suddenly packing a six-gun. Her hair was a mess, she looked disheveled and had stared with her mouth open when he'd mentioned an early morning nature hike.

"Trust me, you won't regret it," he insisted. Maybe it was the promise of good coffee that finally got her to shower and change into outdoor clothes. Wordlessly, he handed her the tall cup of coffee, grabbed the necessary supplies he needed and they were off.

He led her to the sound of waves crashing against unseen

cliff walls.

"You don't have plans on killing me, do you?" were the first words she spoke to him. "Too many people know I'm here with you."

He laughed and hugged her close. "No. Of course not."

"I can't say the same for you," she said completely deadpan. "You deserve to be pushed from these cliffs for waking me up to take a freezing cold hike."

"You wound me."

She slurped her coffee noisily. "If only." But her eyes twinkled and a tiny smile played on her lips.

"Seriously, do you still want to go back?" he asked, surprised by how tense he felt just asking the question.

"Nope. Honest."

He gave her a good-natured squeeze. Something a friend would do. The dense fog muted sound and concealed the distances, but it was like walking in a mystical land. After about fifteen minutes, they stopped.

"Let's stay here," he said, unfolding a small portable chair he'd brought along. He sat in it first, then she sat between his legs and the comforter he'd thrown over her shoulders was used to cover them both.

Out came the thermos of coffee and she drank it as if it were sacred wine. As they drank, they sat appreciating the density of the fog, the dampness that dripped from the trees and muted the sounds of marine and wild life. There was a soulful commune that remained timeless, as if nothing had changed since the first pre-historic fog breathed upon the land.

Would she wait the forty minutes it took for the gift of a new day? It wasn't a sexual thing. It was the first step in sharing the things he loved with her. Maybe that's why he felt a bit nervous. He wondered if she understood how important it was to share this sunrise with her. He wanted to do things like this, or take her to basketball games or the movies.

But maybe she didn't want more than sex. Maybe any minute now, she'd complain that she'd rather be inside. At least she'd stopped shivering and her teeth were no longer chattering.

He waited for her to complain, but she didn't.

In the quiet orchestra, they waited, bundled and warm, reminding James of the day they had shared a bathtub in much the same way.

Little by little, the fog began to dispel, receding like a veil pulled back revealing a breathtaking view. The splendor that spread out before them was just as he'd remembered.

Beautiful!

The sun shyly broke at the horizon, starting the day in virgin hues of melon pink and watercolor lavender, slowly filling the horizon with a spectacular welcome that only the union of ocean and sky could create.

"Oh... James," Sharonda whispered, her voice full of awe.

He kissed her temple, trying not to rub his bristly jaw against her tender skin. A part of him that had been holding its breath seemed to relax. "Stunning, isn't it?"

"Incredible. Thank you." She searched out his hand under the blanket and they held on until the sun warmed their skin and breakfast beckoned.

Epilogue

"Yes, Momma," Sharonda automatically said into the phone. She resisted the urge to sigh as her mother gave her the same you-don't-call-me-you-don't-write-me lecture. Instead, Sharonda toyed with the necklace of rubies James had given her the week before. After a while she busied herself with packing for the weekend, agonizing between the chocolate body paint and the raspberry burn lotion. In the end both went in, along with a few teddies, her robe and—

"Are you listening to me, Ronny?"

"Yes, Momma."

"Old Man Cooper says he saw you with his grandson the other day."

Sharonda cringed. "Ran into him at the elevator."

"Really? Now that's a nice boy, Ronny. He's got himself a job. A fine job. And he's a gentleman too."

Thoughts of the foreplay with James in the elevator left her with only a "mmm-hmm" for a reply.

"He's a church going fella, I'll bet. Used to like music..."

Now he likes wind chimes... And sunrises...

"And he once took me and his mother to play bingo and

cards on crab feed night. Remember that?"

Crab feed? No. Bingo? No. The cards? Oh yeah. Simmer? Yeah. The question was, could she ever forget? Although bingo also sounded promising. "Um, nope, don't remember the crab feed, Momma."

"What kinda car does Jimmy Cooper drive?"

"Don't know—"

"'Cause you can tell a lot about a man by the car he drives. And he's real easy on the eyes, his granpa say."

Sharonda grinned. "Are you matchmaking?"

"Just pointing out a few facts," her mother said defensively. "You probably don't even remember him from church choir. And besides, you could do much worse than James Cooper, you know!"

The raving began again, the matchmaking intentions of her mother's call becoming all the more apparent. Suddenly, Sharonda heard keys and covered the mouthpiece of the phone. When James came into sight, she placed her fingers on her lips to shush him.

Wearing a quizzical expression, he still gave her a brief kiss on the cheek.

"Yes, Momma," Sharonda said, just because her mother seemed to be expecting it.

James looked into her semi-packed suitcase, his eyes resting on the two vibrating balls she had hastily nestled in a silk scarf.

He winked at her and the chimes outside rang, playing their song.

Her mother tried her hand in the matchmaking a bit more before winding down.

James' smile widened and he began removing his silk tie. Once the silver cloth was in his hands, he began to fold, hand over hand in a familiar design.

"Okay, Momma," she replied huskily, trying to pay attention to what she was saying.

"...if you see him, you tell him hi for me. I know he's a painfully shy boy, but like I said, he's a real gentleman..."

"Yes, Momma. I think I got another call. I gotta go."

Her mother sighed, probably realizing the lie. "Okay, Sharonda. You take care and call me sometime, okay sweetie? Oh, and make yourself some lemon-honey tea, dear, you sound like you're about to catch a cold."

"Yes, Momma."

When Sharonda finally hung up, James was shirtless, doing a daring strip tease as he removed his pants, the white shirt. in his hand the silk dragon awaited.

"Oh, James," Sharonda chuckled. "If only my mother could see you now..."

For the first time in her life, she welcomed her mother's matchmaking. Yes, indeed, really, really welcomed it!

Indigo After Dark, Vol. I

By
Nia Dixon and Angelique

Like a musical director who guides an orchestra to a climactic crescendo, Nia Dixon takes you there musically, poetically, and sexually, with her collection of stories, *Midnight Erotic Fantasies*. Her poignant emphasis on female pleasure is told with such awesome detail you'll feel your temperature rising from the first story to the last. She develops a true mixture of erotic fantasies, which will send you running to find pleasure in the arms of the one you love.

In Between the Night by Angelique tells of the erotic adventures of Margaret and her sexual awakening from plain Jane by day to the sensual cat on the prowl, Jade, by night. Margaret is both frightened and intrigued by the dark and dangerous feelings that consume her. It is Anthony, a stranger she meets in the park, who brings out the real woman hidden beneath—and now he, too, is consumed by her fire.

ISBN 1-58571-050-4 $10.95

Order your *Indigo After Dark, Vol. I* today at your favorite bookstore or online at the Genesis Press Web site, www.genesis-press.com.

Indigo After Dark, Vol. II

By

Dolores Bundy & Cole Riley

Brown Sugar Diaries by Dolores Bundy brings you a potpourri of explicit, vividly portrayed erotic short stories that takes an exotic plunge into the vibrant lifestyles of people who go beyond a devotion to unbridled pleasure. Jump into the rhythmic Brazilian nightclub scene with Zoe, a blue-eyed, bronzed temptress whose insatiable lust for sex is sizzling and telling. Her signature song "To Zoe with Love," gives her something she can feel. Travel to Africa with Mandingo Man with Big Feet and discover the mystery behind I got my Mojo working. Fasten your seat belts. These steamy and tantalizing erotic stories are unchained, unleashed and unlimited. And there's more to cum!

The Forbidden Art of Desire by Cole Riley offers a dozen erotic sexcapades featuring people from a variety of backgrounds and circumstances, either in lust or love. In this collection you'll meet a trophy wife who discovers that a threesome with a stranger in Rio has unforeseen benefits for her marriage, a Wall Street career woman who gets more than she bargins for when she orders a special delivery of love, a female cabbie with a penchant for sexual hijinks who finds love in the most unusual situation, a young woman's erotic coming of age at a Parisian bookstore, and many more. In all of these tempting tales, desire is the key ingredient and spark for a sizzling sensual interlude.

ISBN 1-58571-051-2 $10.95
Order your *Indigo After Dark, Vol. II* today at your favorite bookstore or online at the Genesis Press Web site. www.genesis-press.com.

Excerpts from Solstice Offering
Delilah Dawson's
Upcoming Indigo After Dark
Release

GROCERY SHOPPING

"Cleanup on aisle three!" the overhead speaker barked. A young worker moved past me, a mop in his grasp as if it were a gladiator's spear.

I continued pushing my cart down the frozen-food aisle and paused to check on ice cream. Mmm, strawberry, my husband's favorite. Then pistachio, my favorite! I popped my gum as I gave the indecision two seconds of thought. My husband, the inconsiderate, unthinking fool, was most definitely in the doghouse, therefore the ice cream choice was really a no-brainer. I mean, I understand he's a businessman and all, and that he has to travel most of the time, but I hadn't seen him in almost a month! He was supposed to come home today.

But instead he canceled our anniversary dinner.

Still, I sighed and deliberated some more with the door open, wondering if my hips could handle much more decadence. Reluctantly, I started to close the door, catching not only my own frowning reflection but that of a man down the aisle, his gaze fixed intently on me. When the glass door shut, the semi-familiar image disappeared, but now I was too wary to even turn around.

Me? He was looking at me? Maybe that ice cream deserved another look. As casually as possible, I opened the door and checked the reflection for the man again. To my disappointment, the aisle was now clear of any traffic. I turned to check. Gone.

How odd. There had been something sexy in the way he'd been watching me.

I dumped the bucket of my husband's favorite ice cream into my shopping cart, then reminded myself that I could have been dining at the Hyatt if only he hadn't canceled!

The tap-tap-tap made me realize I was drumming my fingers in annoyance. Which also reminded me that I had wasted my time and money getting the perfect manicure just hours ago. I had gone through all that trouble just to impress my man during dinner. My

162

husband likes nails that scratch and leave small marks on him, and I was planning to show him.

The bastard.

I paused by the frozen pizzas, wondering if I should get one. I settled for the pepperoni and was about to close the door when someone moved in from behind me, slipping his hand in and grabbing a box for himself.

"Oh, pardon me," he said quietly, his eyes remaining on mine a few seconds beyond what was considered cordial. It was him! I sucked in air, realizing my heart had picked up an extra beat. His charming smile was framed by his distinguished beard.

That face was familiar, beguiling. I returned the faint smile before deliberately looking away and moving along, not daring to give him a second glance.

We passed each other on aisle six. I didn't even make eye contact; instead I peered at the items before me, pretending I'd never seen so much foot lotion in my life. He cleverly bumped his cart against mine, muttered a deep, rumbled apology and moved a few feet away to look at the prophylactics.

And so we danced...

I grabbed a whisk to examine it.

He grabbed a glass jar of syrupy cherries.

I fondled a bag of walnuts.

He watched me through a jar of honey.

I licked my lips as I tried to decide which can of icing to get.

He made a big deal of sniffing a bottle of chocolate syrup.

Fine.

I stopped, pivoted the squeaky cart and moved on down to squeeze the Charmin.

He moved farther away to size up a large, black, phallic-looking flashlight. Then with a lecherous quirk to his lips, he grabbed some batteries.

Unreasonably annoyed and aroused, I turned away and this time I could've sworn I heard a chuckle as I left.

When I saw him a short distance from me at the deli section, I took my time viewing the large German sausages, the Portuguese linguisa and because I knew he was watching, I grabbed an exquisite ten-inch Italian salami.

Our eyes made contact and his gaze heated. This time he looked away. Feeling cocky, I smirked, dropped the salami into my basket and found myself following him as he stopped at the seafood counter where I watched him buy fresh oysters.

Oysters, my favorite sex food! Myth or not, those suckers could get my juices pumping!

I could hear him discussing cooking instructions with the clerk, the gentle baritone of his voice tugging at me whenever he spoke. I couldn't help but think of my husband and the way he liked to bury his face between my legs and go "oyster tasting," licking and pummeling me with his clever tongue until I was positively incoherent.

I stared blindly at a package of tofu, flushed, and felt a phantom sensual tug in my loins. Blinking several times, I finally realized I was still holding tofu. Tofu?

I put it back and moved away, feeling the man's eyes like a physical caress on my spine.

In the fruit-and-vegetable aisle he brushed past me as I contemplated lettuce, our clothes rustling softly as if apologizing to each other. I felt that brush of him, his clothes, the almost undetectable nudge of his semi-aroused penis. The lingering effect of it almost made me weak.

In the reflective slant of a food guard, I peeked at him, admiring the way he held two small cantaloupes, roughly the same size as my breasts. Locking his gaze with mine, he lifted the fruit to his face and inhaled, bringing a sharp tightness to my nipples, causing them to strain. Those large, firm hands clutched the fruit with the power of a magician, linking the orbs to my breasts. Spellbound, I couldn't look away. Each time his thumb moved over the fruit, I felt it. Even the flicker of his tongue over his lips set my nipples more painfully against my shirt.

I waited, realizing I wanted to be where the fruit was, being touched by his hands and mouth, touched and licked by him, fondled by him....

He turned to add them to his shopping cart, and the spell was broken.

Like bumper cars, we turned and headed in opposite directions.

When he brushed past me again, I was standing by the plums and peaches. With a brief glance in his direction, I lifted the fruit and inhaled its ripeness. The plum looked especially succulent, firm and purple like the head of a stressed erection. I longed to nip the firm flesh, suck on it, taste the juices and feel them in my mouth, my throat.

Peaches are my husband's favorite. Once, long ago, drunk on wine and good soul music, I had halved a refrigerated peach and used it to stroke his length. I sandwiched his penis between the two halves and proceeded to stroke and suckle him simultaneously. Hot mouth, cold fruit. Despite the coolness, his erection had remained and I could see that the fibrous membrane was licking him almost as well as my tongue. I tormented him for a long, long time, loving the helpless way he had begun to groan and thrust, ruining the fruit until it fell apart in my hands. I took the remains and stroked his testicles with it, then licked him clean.

When his fists gripped the sheets in desperation, I whispered that I liked cream with my peaches and within seconds, he grunted and ejaculated in my mouth, chasing the sweet taste of the fruit with his own natural essence.

And yet here I was, my panties getting wet while I drowned in intimate memories.

"Need help with something?" a teenage clerk asked, interrupted my musing. I floundered before I blurted, "No, thanks," in an embarrassingly husky voice.

I could also see that the man who'd been watching had strategically moved to stand behind his cart, but not before I saw his full arousal straining the front of his jeans. With an intense and promising look in my direction, he pushed his cart into another aisle.

I waited about ten seconds before I chased after him. By now my heart was beating wildly, my center had developed a deep pulse, and there was no hiding my extremely perky nipples.

I caught him at the cash register and felt a surge of disappointment. Was our game over so soon? Disheartened, I moved to another open register and waited to be rung up.

I had just reached for my wallet when I glimpsed him again, finding a smile on his face. He winked discreetly at me and I faked a brief wave as if he were my newspaper boy.

The distraction cost me, since now I had several items from our flirting that I certainly did not need. I was juggling the grocery bags in my arms when the whisk tipped over and fell out.

"Allow me." From behind me, the man's voice enveloped me like a scarf.

Feeling like a starstruck teenager, I could only watch as he retrieved it and placed it in my outstretched palm.

"Thanks," I said as my fingers curled around the handle. I suddenly realized he'd tucked a piece of paper in my hand, along with the whisk.

"I'll see you around," he said and headed out of the door with his own grocery bag.

I managed to make it to the car before unfolding the note, which, as it turns out, was really his grocery receipt. On it was a message: Three Palms Inn. Room 177.

I crumpled the note nervously in my fist, then after a few breaths, opened it again and reread it.

Boy, he had nerve! Okay, so maybe I did stroke the thick salami in the deli and fondled the walnuts a bit intimately and...

Hunger for a different kind of salami and walnuts raged through me. I was really, really hungry.

I refused to second-guess myself as I started the car and left the parking lot, headed toward the inn. I was pulling into the parking lot when I saw him entering his room on the ground floor. He paused just slightly to look over his shoulder at me, then went into his room.

I eased into a vacant spot, my hand sweaty on the stick shift. Taking a moment, I inhaled, exhaled, inhaled again. Finally, I decided that if I was going to do this, I had to do it right.

Reclining my seat slightly, I worked my panties over my hips, down my knees and off my ankles. They ended up in a wet heap under my seat, just like my bra. Nervously, I grabbed my purse and irrationally found myself stalling with the car door open. Should I or shouldn't I bring the salami to make a provocative opening remark? Hmmmm.

Nah. I settled for the peaches and threw a couple in my handbag. Then I locked the car, stopped by the nearby ice machine where I found an ice bucket still wrapped in plastic. I filled it with ice, and went straight for Room 177.

After running a hand over my short braids, I knocked on the door. It opened to the gentleman wearing a white robe and an expression that was both mischievous and ardent. His eyes were the same shade of dark cocoa brown as his skin. His lips were full and tempting, his smile pure seduction. For several seconds we let the heat simmer between us as we fully studied each other.

"Come in," he invited, his voice filled with a lover's promise and a spider's threat.

I stepped in and placed the bucket on the small table by the door, barely able to keep my eyes off him. The minute the door closed, I was pulled up against it, his body pressing sensually against mine, letting me know he was absolutely naked and hard beneath the robe.

I dropped my purse and rocked instinctively against his hard-on, catching enough of a breath to meet his mouth-tangling kiss. And that's exactly what it was, our mouths tangling, tongues slipping and curling, tasting, sucking and devouring each other with almost immature finesse. God, I could hardly remember the last time I'd been kissed that way, and I've always loved a moustache, but his conservative beard was a wonderful extra sensation.

With a single move, his hands hungrily roamed over my breasts, then my waist. With his tongue still plunging against mine, I wrapped my legs around his waist.

166

"Christ!" he blasphemed as his hands dropped to clutch my hips. He kissed me again, forcing a slower pace. The wide expanse of his hands slipped lower, moving to my thighs, then under my skirt and upward until his hands held my butt cheeks.

"Sweet," he murmured huskily when he realized I had forgone the underwear. He untied his robe, pulling it open and to the side. Already I could feel the head of his penis intimately introducing itself to me. Hello indeed!

We rocked together in mock thrusts, kissing and nipping our lips while our sexes lubricated on my dripping juices.

I wiggled once, impatiently, and ran my nails over his back. In a confident move, he adjusted his position and slipped into me in one long, hard, fluid motion. I cried out, part pain and the rest an incredulous riptide of pleasurable ripples.

"Ohhh... oh!" I clutched him, riding the spasms that came from being so thoroughly impaled by his shaft. He wasn't extremely thick, but he sure was long! I readjusted ever so slightly, for comfort, for pleasure. His harsh breathing was magnified in the silence. Against my chest, his fingers were busy undoing the buttons of my shirt until the garment hung open.

Then with his hot mouth sucking on my nipples he began to thrust into me, causing my body to thud slightly against the door. I moaned as the vaginal grip sent a sweet spiral up to my womb. Oh, God!

The rhythm was set, in and out, sex to sex, woman to man, until I hardly could think.

His teeth sank into my nipple in a soft bite, his groan trembling on my skin even as he whispered, "Yyyyesssss..."

I don't know if he was trying to hold back, but he suddenly seemed to lose the last of his control and he surged into me, hard, in brief, consecutive power thrusts that strained my thighs.

The final surge came like a roar, hard and overwhelming. His mouth slanted over mine, trembling as I felt his hot semen erupting deep within me.

I clutched him, feeling his legs lock and his buttocks clenching beneath my ankles.

It felt like forever that we stayed there, locked like mating insects, gasping for breath like asthmatic marathoners.

After a while, he seemed to regain strength and without separating, he carried me to the bed where we kissed leisurely for what felt like an endless moment.

He shrugged off his robe then rolled over so I could take off my shirt, then ever so gently, he withdrew his semi-aroused shaft from within me, allowing me to remove my skirt.

Seeing the reflection of the ice bucket in the mirror, I said, "Just a minute," and scrambled off the bed.

I figured he'd earned a free hind shot, so I bent over to dig in my purse for the peaches, then dunked them into the ice bucket, which I placed next to the bed. As I crawled back in, I noticed the bottle of chocolate syrup was on the night table, and the grin on his face was enough to make me chuckle. I guess he'd bought everything he put into his cart as well.

I loved it, being over him and seeing the natural turtleshell shape of the muscles of his abs. He reached for the chocolate syrup and rubbed two perfect rings into my nipples with his fingertips.

Keeping my eyes on his, I reached down and cupped his testicles, feeling the wetness of our release and massaging it into his bulbous weights and hardening cock. Then I moved the peak of my left breast over his waiting mouth, groaning when his teeth nipped my nipple and his lips assuaged the pain in multiple small sucks.

The smell of sex and chocolate filled the air with a sinful decadence, working on my system like fresh-baked pastry at a bakery.

I didn't realize my fist had tightened over his shaft until I heard, "Easy there," and felt his hand cover mine. He sucked my sensitive breast while one hand covered mine over his penis, showing me the rhythm of strokes that he preferred. His other hand found my inner thigh, where my legs straddled one of his.

"Touch me," I whispered even as his fingertips traced my inner thigh, playing with my soft pubic hair. "Inside."

His touch was absolute torment, his fingers slipping between my labia, over my clitoris, stroking and rubbing with minimal penetration. It wasn't until I was jamming my hips against his hand that he began to plunge his thick fingers in, the slick, wet noise of it mixing with my moans when he simultaneously rubbed the heel of his palm on my sensitive clit.

By now my poor nipple was incredibly sensitive, but before I could say anything, he released it and latched on to the other one, giving it equal treatment.

My own pleasure was rolling in so hard and fast that I released his penis, braced my hands on his abs and rocked hard against his hand until I felt like I was melting over him. My voice released a garbled surrendering sound when I finally came, too weak to do anything but slump over him.

168

Breathing hard, he rolled me over onto my back a bit overeagerly. I didn't care. I was feeling drowsy and very satiated. I lifted my tired eyelids and found him licking the tip of his fingers, which had given me so much joy, the fires of desire burning hot in his eyes.

"Mmmm, you taste like wine-cooked oysters."

I smiled weakly and closed my eyes, but I could feel the bed shifting as he moved about. In truth, I wasn't expecting to feel his hands spread my thighs, nor to feel his mouth French-kissing my finger-romped vagina.

"Oohh," I complained weakly, "it's so sensitive. Please"

"I'm getting mine," he growled and continued the oral plundering as if I had hidden a treasure that he intended to recover with his tongue. His beard was wonderfully stimulating¾soft, ticklish, erotic. It wasn't long after that I was no longer complaining, but instead I was gripping the bed sheet in one hand and his head in the other.

Every lick and suck was so sensitive... so utterly sensitive...

"Pleeeease," I whispered.

"Yes," he agreed, and with a panther-like move he was over me, thrusting slow and long until he was sheathed completely inside me.

"Oh my," I whimpered in shameless delight.

His reply was a low, carnal grunt as me moved again, and again and again... Over and over, becoming harder thrusts, until the bed rocked, my breasts jiggled and I felt his rough ejaculation ripping through him. He fell on me, clutching me hard as the remaining shudder overcame him.

With his remaining strength, he cupped my buttocks and rolled over so as not to crush me. Minutes slipped by where all we did was catch our breath and listen to it until it became more even.

Entwined, with our flesh perspiring and semi-sticky, we rested and fell asleep.

I don't know why I awoke with a start, but I noticed that the alarm clock on the side table said I'd slept for about half an hour. The man was snoring softly, so I went to the bathroom and took a quick shower. It felt positively indecent to dress without my underwear, but I was really liking it.

As I stepped back into the room, I saw him propped on his side, waiting for me.

"You're leaving?" he asked.

"Yes, I have to go."

He just watched, his eyes eloquent.

"But there is one thing I forgot to do," I said and stepped back into the bathroom. I soaked a hand towel in warm water and took it with me to the bedside, to where his penis was once again tenting up the sheets.

"Lay back and enjoy," I said as I threw back the sheets to wash his phallus. When that was done, I reached into the ice bucket for a peach and used a plastic knife to cut it in half, removing the pit.

"What are you doing?" he asked gruffly.

"Having some peaches and cream," I replied saucily, giving him a wink.

"Are you keeping your clothes on?"

"Yup."

He grinned devilishly and settled more comfortably on the bed, parting his thighs for our mutual convenience. He even padded some pillows behind his back and head for a better view.

I grabbed the two juicy halves, positioned myself between his legs and touched them to the base of his cock.

His sharp hiss cut the silence as he tried to shrink away from the cold but his hips and cock remained thrusting outward. I rubbed the syrupy halves up and down his length, over the ridges of his eager stalk, circling the tip of his penis then down to the base, letting the fibrous membranes brush against his testicles. His erection went down, but not entirely.

"Cup the fruit in your hands," he commanded weakly and I did, making a virtual peach vagina where he thrust again and again. Soon the power of his thrusts smashed the fruit and all that was left was my wet hands on his penis, but I was already moving my mouth to catch the dribbling syrup. It was delicious, tasting of the warmth of his skin and the coolness of the fruit.

I licked and nipped, cleaning up the fruit and gobbling noisily. My thumb followed my plundering mouth. Cresting the ridge of his ejaculatory path, I saw the sinews of his thighs tighten and strain with need.

"The peach was delicious," I murmured, using his penis like a microphone. "May I have some cream with it?"

"Yesss." He grasped my head and thrust into my mouth with a surrendering groan, filling the back of my throat with hot semen. I swallowed it greedily, licking whatever dripped over my lips and trailed on my chin. I held him there, in my warm oral kiss until the pulse of his penis became faint and soft.

I straightened, trying to ignore the orange stain on the front of my pristine white shirt and the heavy moisture between my thighs.

He looked so content, so defeated, so satisfied.

I bent over and kissed him. "Good-bye."

He reached for me. "Wait¾"

"I have to go," I said. He watched me for a minute before nodding.

I blew him a kiss and left, feeling wanton, crazy and as much a sensual woman as I'd felt in quite some time.

When I finally pulled up to my driveway, I was feeling warm from the memory. I sat behind the steering wheel, reliving the great details before finally prompting myself to throw my underwear into my purse, grab my groceries and head for the front door.

My keys hadn't even touched the door when the man's car parked behind mine and he stepped out, also grabbing his groceries. For an instant, our gazes connected and we shared a slow smile of lovers, of friends.

"There was an extra peach left," he said, the tone of his voice making me shamelessly aware of my lack of undergarments.

"Mmm, lucky you," I replied.

"Yeah. I kinda enjoyed the torture." His long stride brought him to me, but I focused on unlocking the door.

I stepped inside, with him half a step behind me. By his breath upon my neck, I could tell he'd been about to nibble on my ear when¾

"SURPRISE!" Several people shouted at once. "HAPPY ANNIVERSARY!"

I was so stunned I almost dropped the groceries.

"Mom! Dad!" my daughter exclaimed as she walked toward us. Christ! Everyone was there-neighbors, friends!

"Dad, you were supposed to keep her away for only half an hour. Where were you guys? You're late! "

"Stuff happens," he said with a noncommittal shrug. I turned toward my husband to yank on his skewered necktie. Oh, I could've strangled him!

My ever-inquisitive daughter looked into my husband's grocery bag. "A flashlight? Cherries and¾"

"Well," I interrupted, "if I'm going to mingle, I should at least refresh myself."

My daughter placed the bag on the counter and reached for mine, leaving me no choice but to surrender it to her insistent hands.

"Mom, are you not wearing a bra?" My daughter gasped indelicately, her whispered mortification turning into a blush on her cheeks. Oh, great! I wondered who else had overheard.

"The strap broke," I lied lamely.

My husband came to the rescue by taking my hand and leading me away while instructing my daughter. "Sweetie, would you entertain while your mother and I go upstairs to change. We'll be down shortly."

We practically raced up the stairs, reluctantly falling back into our roles as parents and party hosts.

"Happy anniversary, love," he whispered, flashing me a smile that I never tired of seeing.

"Ditto," I replied, squeezing his hand. I was glad that I'd picked his favorite ice cream after all. And the peaches and...

I really have to go shopping more often!

ORDER FORM

Mail to: Genesis Press, Inc.
315 3rd Avenue North
Columbus, MS 39701

Name _____

Address _____

City/State _____ Zip _____

Telephone _____

Ship to (if different from above)

Name _____

Address _____

City/State _____ Zip _____

Telephone _____

Qty.	Author	Title	Price	Total

Use this order form, or call 1-888-INDIGO-1	Total for books $ _____
	Shipping and handling: $4 first two book, $1 each additional books $ _____
	Total S & H $ _____
	Total amount enclosed $ _____

Mississippi residents add 7% sales tax

ORDER FORM

Mail to: Genesis Press, Inc.
315 3rd Avenue North
Columbus, MS 39701

Name _____

Address _____

City/State _____ Zip _____

Telephone _____

Ship to (if different from above)

Name _____

Address _____

City/State _____ Zip _____

Telephone _____

Qty.	Author	Title	Price	Total

Use this order form, or call 1-888-INDIGO-1	Total for books $ _____

	Shipping and handling:
	    $4 first two book, $1 each
	    additional books $_____

	Total S & H $ _____
	Total amount enclosed $ _____

Mississippi residents add 7% sales tax

ORDER FORM

Mail to: Genesis Press, Inc.
315 3rd Avenue North
Columbus, MS 39701

Name _____

Address _____

City/State _____ Zip _____

Telephone _____

Ship to (if different from above)

Name _____

Address _____

City/State _____ Zip _____

Telephone _____

Qty.	Author	Title	Price	Total

Use this order form, or call 1-888-INDIGO-1	Total for books $ _____
	Shipping and handling: $4 first two book, $1 each additional books $ _____
	Total S & H $ _____
	Total amount enclosed $ _____

Mississippi residents add 7% sales tax

ORDER FORM

Mail to: Genesis Press, Inc.
315 3rd Avenue North
Columbus, MS 39701

Name _____

Address _____

City/State _____ Zip _____

Telephone _____

Ship to (if different from above)

Name _____

Address _____

City/State _____ Zip _____

Telephone _____

Qty.	Author	Title	Price	Total

Use this order form, or call 1-888-INDIGO-1	Total for books $ _____
	Shipping and handling: $4 first two book, $1 each additional books $ _____
	Total S & H $ _____
	Total amount enclosed $ _____
	Mississippi residents add 7% sales tax